MW00873754

Books by Mary Mead

Monarch Beach Series
Out of the Blue (Book 1)
Wild Blue Yonder (Book 2)
Bluebonnets (Book 3)
Deep Blue See (Book 4)

Hot Storage

www.MaryMeadBooks.com

Out of the Blue

A Monarch Beach Mystery
(Book 1)

By Mary Mead

© 2013, 2018 Mary E. Mead

Chapter One

Let me say right up front I am NOT crazy.

I may be a little unusual, but given the circumstances, I am entitled to be a little off center. Bear with me and I'll tell you what happened. You make up your own mind.

I don't eat the crayons or hide marmalade in my armpits. I don't see dead people. I am a licensed driver and a registered voter.

You want crazy? Anatidaephobia. Now that's crazy. That's the fear that somewhere, somehow, a duck is watching you. Who would admit that, even to their doctor?

My name is Thomasina Joseffa Bishop, which is enough to shove anyone a few degrees off center. I was half way through second grade before I could spell it. By third grade I went by Tee, or Teejay, to the relief of my teachers.

I am also a survivor. That means I get to wear a purple shirt at every Relay for Life event, having earned the right by surviving cancer.

If you want to kill a conversation quicker than spilled wine on the heirloom table cloth, say one word – cancer. Admit you had it, and folks will back up a good four feet and start looking for the exit, in case you might be exhaling cancer cells right at them. Even close friends may suddenly decide to visit Cancun, or at least give the impression they may have moved.

About the only phone calls coming your way are reminders of doctor appointments or a telemarketer wanting to sell you something and they will hang up on you if you mention cancer, in case it might sneak down the telephone wire and infect them through their ear.

Cancer is the 'do or die' disease – do what the doctor says or die. It is the red wolf, tearing you apart, wearing you down, rendering you weaker and weaker until you are too tired to fight and succumb to its lethal bite.

No one is exempt.

It is the equal opportunity offender. Democrat or Republican, black, white or purple, male or female, makes no difference. Each one must run the gauntlet alone, a private and personal battle, fought in silence.

Chemotherapy is poison, literally. A series of chemicals that poisons the cancer cells and kills them. Sadly, it also kills a lot of healthy cells, at times it will make you question yourself and your doctors, to wonder if it's worth it.

Radiation therapy is painless but as relentless as the wolf itself, and brings its own set of side effects. You will begin with a full plastic mask of your head, face first, a mask extending back like Nefertiti's crown. The mask is used to clamp your head to a table, for your own safety, so there is no possibility you can move. You are lucky if you can manage to blink.

The technicians warn you that some patients may experience a flash of blue light or smell ozone and there is nothing to worry about with either effect.

With your head clamped down, the table is raised up, everyone leaves the room and a machine that looks like something from Star Wars begins to hum and then it starts to move, slowly curving over you, left to right and back again.

In my case, there was a flash of blue, inside my head, a mental flash seen behind closed eyelids. A brilliant blue, like the clear summer sky straight over head, not the lighter color near the horizon. There was a very strong smell of ozone that filled my head..

Treatments only last fifteen minutes or so. Once the machine turns off, the staff comes back in, lowers the table, releases your mask, and you sit up. Done.

No smell, no blue, all over.

A cubby is marked with your name on a piece of tape and it is here you replace your mask, grab your clothes and get dressed. After the first few treatments, which are daily, five days in a row, weekends off, you know what to expect and the bright blue flash and the smell won't bother you any more.

To this day I can smell lightning from a mile away, even if I can't see it. One of those little side effects I got to keep after treatment.

Side effects are another leg of the race. They vary from patient to patient and cannot be predicted or explained.

Hair loss is the most common. In my case, I was bald as a bowling ball for two years but still had to shave my legs. No one ever said cancer was fair.

Other changes you may encounter include being cold all the time, your body temperature dropping five or six degrees. Doesn't sound like much until you think about a temperature of 102, about four degrees above average and that's a whopping fever.

Heavy sweaters, sweatshirts and thick socks are your new best friends and quilts are worth their weight in gold.

Your tastes will likely change. Former favorites may taste like gasoline, which can be okay since they will come back up still warm. A good rug in front of the porcelain throne may help keep your fanny warm while making your donations.

There are other side effects, like I said, they vary from one to another. Survive and most will fade into faint memories. Some may remain, permanent additions to the new you. These, too, vary from patient to patient.

~~~

As you may have noticed, mental illness is NOT a side effect, a point in my favor.

There is so much technical and medical knowledge involved in treating cancer, the average person will never understand it. Even radiation oncologists don't know all the side effects to brain radiation, which is often a follow up procedure to chemo.

Chemotherapy tried to kill me before the cancer could, landing me in intensive care at the hospital the first week of treatment. Doctors, nurses, ambulance rides, hospitals, even blood transfusions were added to my treatment.

Months of being poked, prodded, stuck with needles, more needles embedded in my arm, the backs of my hands, for hours on end, day after day.

Set apart, too sick to eat, sometimes too sick to care.

About this time I added my own peculiar side effect. Tim showed up.

I have no clue exactly when he showed up, he just did. Yes, I said he.

I hear his voice inside my head. It's not my voice, not even close. His is deeper, with a Southern drawl, and a warm feel, like caramel on chocolate.

Let's say your friend calls you on the phone. Perfectly normal, happens a million times a day, right? You hear them clearly, in your ear, inside your head. No one questions it, or considers it unusual. It's a simple phone call.

I hear Tim's voice the same way. In my head. I just do it without benefit of a phone. Blue flash, ozone, and Tim is there. Due to those special effects, I tend to think he was born of radiation treatments but I have nothing to back up that belief.

It is strictly one way, Tim to me. I can't call him. I've tried. I can't predict when he will show up. He just does. Blue flash, ozone smell and he has announced his presence.

I asked my doctors about it and that earned me referrals to the staff psychiatrist, whose main job was explaining your final days. She had no experience with voices as a side effect and suggested I move on to another branch of medicine.

I declined and stopped asking.

I like Tim.

I enjoy his company, enjoy not being alone all the time. He became a part of my life so the heck with the psych crew, I kept him.

We talk of many things, no cabbages but sometimes kings. We like the same movies, and mostly the same books, which we can discuss for hours. He doesn't cost anything to keep – I don't have to feed him or clean up after him. What more could you ask?

He calls me Muse because he says I inspire him. Not sure what I inspire him to do but I've been called worse in my forty years on the planet so I'm good with it.

Did I name him Tim? I don't think so. I think he told me his name somewhere in the beginning but I can't give you a specific instance.

There you have it.

Me and Tim.

My personal side effect, the one that might possibly come down on the side of mentally unstable, or in laymen's terms, crazy.

The thing is, you won't know if I'm talking to him or not, so how can you judge? I could be talking to him right this minute for all you know. The doctors faced the same problem and dropped it from my medical records. I think the psychiatrist suggested it.

~~~

The lung cancer diagnosis was the hardest part. Most of us who receive that bit of news react the same way – tears, cussing and realizing if you are at a bank robbery you can step up and take the bullet.

Then treatment begins and so does the race. Against time, and the red wolf who will stay right on your heels in case you falter.

My dedicated medical teams did not fail.

My life was saved.

The expense was enormous.

I lost everything.

My job, my home, my savings and sixty pounds. My boss couldn't hold my job, the bank couldn't hold my home without payments and the pharmacy sucked up my savings with a giggle. My insurance company paid a lot, not nearly enough, and was so happy I survived they dropped me.

I was assured the weight would return, with my hair, and encouraged to eat lots of protein. I was also warned that the cancer could return at any time. The time between my doctor's appointments would gradually decrease. The threat of a return was my little gift.

Underweight and destitute but, by golly, alive.

An aunt stepped in and gave me a place to live. She owned a property here in town, with three rental houses on one lot. She installed me in one and charged me with keeping the others rented, the property clean and in good repair.

Included in my duties was the care and feeding of two cats, Cletus and Dave, left behind by a previous tenant. My aunt was a dog person. Didn't like cats.

She didn't like animal abuse more.

When the abused and abandoned animals were discovered, she had them vet checked, neutered, shot, chipped, bathed and fed.

Once deemed healthy they moved into the house with me and under my care.

I'm okay with them. It took days for them to come out from under the bed, even longer for them to stay in a room with me but since I was also the giver of cat food, they gradually accepted me.

Now they sleep on the bed with me, Cletus curled behind my knees, Dave snuggled against my feet.

They are not allowed outside so they depend on me for food, water and a clean cat box.

In turn, I've become attached to both of them. It's comforting to curl up with them, to drift to sleep to the sound of their purring.

And there you have it.

Neighborhood cat lady? Yes.

Survivor? Yes.

Crazy? No.

A little off the mark, but you can't prove it.

~~~

Having done her familial duty my aunt was off to Europe, leaving me to my new position as property manager and cat care supervisor. A team of attorneys handle her affairs in her absence, and I report to them.

My duties include keeping the other two houses rented, the grounds clean and neat, and taking care of any necessary repairs. The attorneys set up a charge account at the local hardware store, gave me petty cash for minor expenditures and manage the bank account where I deposit collected rents.

Anything else comes up, I have to contact them.

My assets are twelve boxes of books and a wardrobe of sweats, sweaters, thick wool socks that I knitted as part of my recovery routine, and jeans.

I have my computer and a printer. There is also my Kindle, my chief form of entertainment.

After a year of being poked, stuck, prodded, rolled around, radiated, and told what to do, I have become accustomed to being alone. I'm used to it. I kind of like it.

Now no one wakes me at two a.m. to take my temperature, check my vitals, or give me a pill. If I wake at night the sounds I hear are the wind, the nearby surf or the cats playing in the dark.

Dave has a thing for floor hockey, played by taking anything he can lift into the kitchen and batting it around until it slides under the fridge and can no longer be retrieved.

Cleaning under there is a lot like Christmas, you never know what you're going to get.

When I was at home during those months I didn't wear a scarf, although I owned two dozen in varying colors. That's a necessity when you're a bald woman. Men get away with it just fine, women get stared at.

My hair is slowly growing back, in a different color. Before cancer I had auburn hair and now I'm a blond. I've been told this is a common occurrence. One survivor I know was bald at forty, had cancer at forty five, and by fifty had a full head of black curly hair. His wife loves it.

I still wear a scarf once in a while, although my hair has grown back to an inch or so in length. There's a halo, a pure white circle of hair, right on the crown of my head. I resist suggestions to dye it, considering it a badge of merit. I earned it.

It's hair. You go bald for a couple of years and you'll understand.

I am a reader. In desperate times, I've been known to read the back of the cereal box. That's a joke. I have no problem re-reading books I have enjoyed and I own enough of them that I have never been that desperate.

I found it difficult to hold a book during chemo. They were either too heavy or too awkward with a needle in the back of my hand. I had looked at the e-readers, digital books, before I got sick and declined.

With my difficulty holding books, I reconsidered and bought a Kindle.

Now I wonder how I lived without it.

Like many others I hate to see so many bookstores closed across the country due to the digital tomes. At the same time, I loved the ease of downloading a new book, at any hour, not being subject to set days and times.

I can browse books at three a.m. if I choose.

Although I read a lot of different genres my favorites are mysteries, the gentle kind, not the gory, explicit ones. I like to think it keeps my mind active figuring out who done it or why. I love the puzzles. Plus, some of my best friends are fictional, like Spenser and Hawk, or Elvis Cole and Joe Pike.

They can get gritty but you know you're safe when those guys are around.

I admit to being nosy, whether it's my preferred reading material or just genetics. I am that woman. You know, the one who watches the whole neighborhood.

Okay, maybe not the whole neighborhood, just my two charges, the two houses that face mine. My aunt's rules are simple: small pets are allowed with prior approval, visitors are asked to park on the street and not block the drive, and rents are due on the first. There is a ten day grace period, after which a late fee is added as a penalty.

There are no exceptions.

I consider it part of my job to keep an eye on the tenants, making sure they obey the rules and to watch over the grounds.

My aunt has entrusted this property to me. I keep a close eye on both of my rental units and the neighborhood around us. I think it's just a naturally inquisitive nature. Or like I said at first, I may just be nosy.

I'm entitled. I'm a survivor.

~~~

The property is rectangular with a central driveway splitting it in half. My house sits on one side, the other two houses on the opposite side, facing mine.

The main house, mine, faces the street, although windows both up and downstairs watch over the other two homes, from across the main driveway.

A retired school teacher lives in the rear house, smallest of the three, the one facing the rear portion of my side which is undeveloped.

Miss Ellie is writing the great American novel in her spare time, her prime time being taken up with gardening and cooking. She spends her mornings growing it, using the undeveloped section of my rear lot, for her extended gardening.

She spends the afternoon harvesting and cooking the results. I benefit from her efforts as she usually makes too much and shares it, often shows up at my back door with homemade soups and casseroles that are easy to warm up.

Next door to her, separated by a hedge, and facing my house is a mirror image of mine. Two story, two bedrooms, a bath and linen closet upstairs: living room, kitchen, dining room and half bath downstairs.

Mine also features a working fireplace downstairs, in the living room. When a fire is crackling away it helps to warm my bedroom, directly above. The front door is flanked by built in bookcases which are kept fully loaded.

In case technology or internet connections fail.

Through my kitchen window I often watch John Kincaid, the occupant right across the drive from me. Our windows face each other. When I am doing dishes I am looking directly from my kitchen window into his kitchen window.

I know from his application that he is a police officer, rank of detective, my age, single. He is a big man, over six feet, with rust colored hair, brown eyes, and very handsome.

The personal information is on the application he filled out to rent the house. The physical description is from my own observations through the kitchen window.

Also on the form, tucked in my filing cabinet, is his annual income. I know he can afford the place, and so far, he has always paid on time.

My only reservation was his looks, that he might be the guy with a parade of women. I didn't want to deal with cat fights or jealous women hanging around, trying to get a glimpse of him.

The fact that an officer of the law lives right on the property is a good selling point should I need one. I know Miss Ellie loves living next door to a cop.

Being John's landlady has another perk - the single gals all want the dirt on the hunk. Sally, one of the waitresses at Kelly's diner, gives me free coffee so she can ask about him. As the town's crier she wants any scrap of information she can root out.

Sadly, I have no nuggets for her.

He goes to work, he comes home. The only female I ever saw at his home was his sister Jessica, who introduced herself when she arrived for a visit and he wasn't home.

While he is always pleasant when we cross paths, at the same time he is always a little distant.

I figure as a cop, and a detective at that, he has other things on his mind.

~~~

As suddenly as it starts, it ends. You're cured. You have won this round. Actually, in my case, I didn't even think about it. It just happened. It was a case of oh, look, no doctors this week, or next week, and it stretched into months. I must be getting better.

Even now, over a year later, I consider cancer the enemy. I did not win the fight. I survived this battle. I live with the knowledge that at any time, the next battle may begin. Such knowledge does not make a comfortable pillow.

The cats fit very well with my situation.

Dave, smallest of the boys, is a typical cat - into everything. Almost every morning starts with picking up something he has retrieved from somewhere he didn't belong and claimed as his own.

Anything from my truck keys, to a spoon, to my watch can be found in the kitchen where he has been playing hockey. He still owes me a watch that has never resurfaced.

Cletus is the shy one. Somewhere along the line his tail had been cut off, leaving just a small stub and a large fear of people. Slightly larger than Dave, he is the follower. Where Dave goes Cletus is a cautious caboose, often giving away Dave's location by crouching nearby.

Dave is the proud owner of an extra- long tail that also gives him away when he attempts to hide under a cushion or a sweat shirt he has pulled off on the floor. Between his tail and his brother, it's pretty hard for Dave to hide successfully.

Since the cats can't go outside they chase one another all over the house, up and down the stairs, around corners, under tables and where ever I am about to step. Both have the knack of getting right in front of me and slowing down, or laying down to impede my progress.

We adjusted to each other and get along. They were the first warm creatures inside my me bubble, the place that has been my sole home for over a year. We went from toleration to affection in just a few months.

Well, I went to affection. I can't speak for the boys.

The house and its surroundings suit me, and the cats, just fine.

I am paid a small salary by the law firm that handles my aunt's affairs. It comes in the mail on the first of every month, to the cat's relief I'm sure, as they are firmly convinced my sole purpose in life is to see to their feeding.

While it is enough to get us by there were times I missed the urgency of having a job, a place to go at a specific time, not to mention the means to buy those little extras that come up, such as books.

Books are a necessity.

To that end a few months ago I contacted a couple of small businesses I had worked with before cancer - doing their accounting and payroll, paying their bills, doing taxes at the end of the year.

Together we worked out a schedule. I work on a monthly retainer, mostly online, and we get along fine. They don't have to hire another employee and I don't have someone looking over my shoulder.

With my two accounts I am able to get a little ahead. The workload is not overwhelming, it doesn't demand full time and yet it still supplements my income. I am not rich, or likely to become so, but I have enough that I don't worry.

In my family, books are counted as members. We all read. We share books, recommend books, and buy books for each other as a matter of course. Favorite books are read and re read, time and again, and given preference on the book cases that abound in every home.

I wanted to read an old favorite a few months ago, one that I didn't own. The library didn't have a copy.

Checking on Amazon to see if they had a copy available, I discovered that more than half of the books residing beside the front door had resale value.

I amused myself all afternoon listing some of them. The next morning, my email said I had two sales that needed to be shipped immediately.

I had discovered online selling

That was the start of my online business, selling used books. I am not the only one who remembers and enjoys a lot of the older books. Due to space limits, many libraries discard old favorites, like Rex Stout, Erle Stanley Gardner, and other great mystery writers from the forties and fifties.

From these first few sales I realized that the more inventory I had, the more money I can make. To that end I go to thrift shops, yard and garage sales, even the rummage sales at the churches.

I have even made a few contacts with local dealers.

One of those dealers, Andy Casellas, took the time to teach me a few things, loaned me some books on antiques and generally helped on this new career. Gradually I added a few collectibles, such as hand crocheted doilies and tablecloths, a few antique pieces of glass.

As my knowledge grows, so does his trust in me. Several times he has hired me to run the shop while he goes to shows, giving me more experience in identifying the good stuff and a chance to make a little more money.

While I am not rich I am a lot more secure.

I invested in a smart phone and learned to use it. With the phone I can check prices, availability and other details online without having to make lists and check later.

Andy is on speed dial. I can send a picture of an item and he can text back yay or nay so I don't buy quite as many duds.

I am nowhere near an expert, but learning every day.

The profit margin is enough to make it worth the effort.

Cancer had cut me out of the herd. Online selling is my ticket back, getting into the social swing, meeting people, and getting out. More important, I have begun to let a few people inside, my boundaries widening, allowing more space in my world.

Some of my remaining friends meet up at The Gem, the local watering hole, on Friday nights. The actual name of the bar is The Gem of the Coast. Too pretentious for the locals, over time it was shortened to just The Gem.

This also has the added advantage of telling people you are going to The Gem which sounds like the gym and gives the impression you are health conscious and fit.

Sharon Kelly is my best friend. She has been in that position since kindergarten. At her insistence I began to join her at the Gem several times a month.

It seemed a little strange at first, to be out with people instead of huddled up with a book and the cats.

After a while I began to look forward to it. The Gem is informal, jeans and boots, awash in country music and beer. Everyone danced with everyone else, and before long I overcame my reluctance and was dancing with whoever asked.

Monarch Beach is a small town. Some say the city limit signs are posted on the same pole. I know the people. If I don't know them personally, I know someone who does. The locals at the Gem were people I have known most of my life.

I drive a Ford Explorer, bought BC, before cancer, that is an older model and paid for in full.

It is roomy enough for boxes and larger purchases so I can carry quite a bit if needed. My hunt for yard sales, rummage sales and the like depends on local newspapers, the signs tacked on telephone poles, taped to cars and trucks, and ads from local schools and churches posted in the grocery store.

Friday, Saturday and Sunday, weather permitting, are hunting days. The rest of the week I am indoors, sorting, cataloging and researching, packing and shipping.

I rarely entertain so the dining room is now an office of sorts. I found a small desk that just fits in the corner by the window. The dining room table often doubles as the wrapping and shipping department.

There are a lot of people out there supplementing income with yard sales, garage sales, and online selling. Thrift stores are thriving, the local swap meet is packed during the warmer months. We all love a bargain and the recent economy hit everyone, no one is immune to a little extra cash.

It gets to be like a game. If I see something interesting, I can check online instantly with my phone, send a picture to Andy to get his opinion. If all else fails, I gather things that I like having in my home. A lot of my decor is pre-owned. I haven't bought anything new for quite a while.

With my Kindle for reading, the cats, and Tim, for company, the little business on the side doing well, I am comfortable and content. I do a good job for my Aunt Johnnie, I enjoy my feline roommates and my little sideline business keeps me busy.

See? Common as dirt. Crazy? No. If you ignore my relationship with Tim, I am as normal as table salt.

Chapter Two

Last month started out as usual.

On Monday morning I pulled on some sweats and sneakers and headed for the beach for a walk. Our best weather is after Labor Day. The days are still long and golden, the throngs of tourists are gone, except for the surge at Thanksgiving, they won't return till spring. The beach is ours again at one of the most beautiful times of the year.

That early morning the beach was sparsely populated with other walkers and joggers, each in their own little world, moving along in both directions at various speeds, nodding to each other, the occasional smile, enjoying the sound of the surf, the cries of the gulls, the fresh salty air coming in on the breeze.

Just beyond the breakers a few surfers bobbed like strange black birds, waiting for the right wave. Along the shore a black and white dog chased the flock of sandpipers that raced back and forth in the shallow foam of flattened waves, the muted thunder of the breakers provided the background music.

Above, the gulls circled, skreeling among themselves, always looking for a morsel along the water line.

I used that time to organize my day, making little mental notes of things that needed to be done. I liked watching the water swirl and shift, hearing the sand whisper to the tide, picking up the pretty pebble or piece of shell.

The pockets of my sweat shirts have a tendency to house little treasures I pick up and hope to remember to remove before doing the laundry.

Good exercise, at the same time refreshing and relaxing, a good start to the day, and a little extra boost for my memory which needs all the help it can get.

Tim had not made an appearance for several days. I tried calling him in my mind which has never worked. One of those things. He has complete control over our conversations. Whether it's a mental aberration, a split personality, whatever, he gets to choose when to pop in. When he doesn't, I miss him.

The weekend had yielded several boxes of books to sort and a landscape print that might have some value. If not, it fit my rather unique decor and I was thinking about where to hang it when I noticed a big, dark roll of something in the surf. Washed in so far onto the beach that its weight was keeping it from washing back out to sea.

West coast beaches are often foggy or overcast in the mornings, washing the colors into varying shades of gray which often make it difficult to see what's in the water.

Dead seals and sea lions have washed up, beautiful strange shaped logs reported to be from Japan, all sorts of flotsam and jetsam dot our shore, especially after a storm.

This was something bigger than usual, what could definitely be a large, dead seal. As I got closer, right up to the foamy edge of the surf, I could see that is was, indeed, a body. Not a seal.

It looked human.

I looked around to see if anyone else noticed. The surfers floated beyond the breakers, looking out to sea. Two people further down the beach huddled into their jackets, heads close together.

The last push of the tide had turned the body and shoved it further onto the beach where it was now stuck in the shallow wash of receding waves, too heavy to wash back out.

Several gulls swooped close and I swung my arm at them.

There were no eyes, just sand filled gaps where they used to be. A pale lump with shreds floating and dangling represented the nose. The teeth were exposed, no lips to cover them.

Small sweeps of salt water washed around the corpse where it rested now in the shallow foam, attracting the interest of the gulls.

Feeling the cold water wash over my feet broke the spell and I stepped back out of the water that crept up around me.

I backed away and splashed my way up to the firmer sand.

I felt no urge to scream, just a terrible sadness.

I pulled my phone from my pocket.

My 911 call went from sheriff to state ranger to beach patrol. While I waited for their arrival, two surfers finally noticed and came in to join me. Sticking their boards into the softer sand, they splashed back to the body, and took up a stance between the body and the surf, keeping it from going back out to sea.

One looked back at me and shook his head, like I had expected CPR or something.

21

The hissing foam of the flattened waves still washed around the feet but the body hadn't moved much since I first saw it. It had washed up as far as it was going to go.

A jogger slowed and joined our small group. We stood around with folded arms, the chilly breeze off the water adding to the funereal atmosphere. We spoke quietly if at all. My feet were cold from the wet sneakers.

The beach ranger was the first to arrive, grabbing his walkie-talkie immediately, calling in and talking in some number jargon none of us understood, the crackling response no more clear.

He splashed out in the shallow water and joined the surfers standing between the waves and the body although it still hadn't moved.

Five minutes later the rescue unit pulled up in a spray of sand and our small group backed away, moving up into the softer dry sand.

Two uniformed men hopped out of the ambulance, one trotted to join the surfers guarding the body and the other opened the back of the vehicle. I watched him pull on latex gloves and remove a body board, covered in some kind of heavy plastic, which he carried to those by the body.

The shallow wavelets spread over and around their shoes as they conferred.

Surprisingly gentle, the men worked as a team and carefully rolled the body onto the board, pulling the edges of the plastic up and tucking it in. Once it was loaded to their satisfaction, they lifted and carried it up to the hard packed sand, where they placed it close to the ambulance.

Then we all waited around for the police department, whose representative arrived in an unmarked silver pickup, wearing jeans and a sweat shirt. He lifted the shirt to show the gold badge clipped to his belt when he joined the others.

The official party gathered around the bundle on the board while the rest of us stood to the side like a colony of penguins, none of us willing to leave the scene, all of us wondering who it was while hoping it was no one we knew.

We exchanged cautious remarks in low voices while we watched. The rescue squad shuffled around in the wet sand, taking pictures, talking softly.

I was surprised to see that the guy with the badge on his jeans was John Kincaid, my renter, the one who lived right across the drive from me.

He was moving around the surfers, back and forth with the guys at the rescue vehicle, making notes on a small tablet.

When he glanced back at our group he caught my eye. I could see he recognized me about the same time I realized who he was. He said something to one of the uniforms and then made his way across the sand to where I huddled in the freshening sea breeze.

"How you doing?" he greeted me, "are you the one who called it in?"

"Yes, sir," I said. Officials always made me nervous even if I do collect their rent.

"Bishop, right?" He had his little pad out and was writing things down. His pen paused as he waited for my answer.

"Yes, sir," I answered.

He smiled at me, and dropped the hand holding the tablet. "Must have been a little unsettling, huh?"

I nodded.

"Want to tell me what happened?"

I stammered out my story while I avoided looking at the group around the body.

"Did you see anyone else near here? A boat? Anything?"

"No, sir. I thought at first it was a log, or a seal or something. I called 911 when I realized it was a body."

He lifted the notebook and made a couple of notes.

"How about sounds? Did you hear anything?"

I shook my head. "The surf, you know? I was just walking along, not paying much attention."

"Okay, then," he pulled a business card from the back of his notebook, wrote on it and handed it to me. "If you think of anything else, or something comes to you later, give me a call." He indicated what he had written on the card. "That's my cell phone number. You can reach me any time."

I tucked the card into my back pocket.

"I know where you live and your phone number," he continued. "I'll call if I need anything else. Or walk across the drive."

He reached out and patted my shoulder. "Ugly way to start the day. I'm sorry it had to be you who found it. Hope the rest of your day is better."

With that he turned and made his way back to the group near the ambulance.

I knew he was a detective, from his rental agreement. Now, watching him take charge of the situation and give orders I had a new respect for my renter. Somehow he looked bigger in his official capacity.

I was used to seeing him under different conditions, like when he dropped off his rent check, or waved as he drove down the drive. I had extended casual invitations to join me when he commented on how good the barbecue smelled, or the smells coming from my kitchen but he always declined so we had no real interaction.

This was the first time I had really looked at him. I mean looked at him as a man. No wonder the ladies of Jade Beach wanted dirt on this guy. He had an air about him, confidence maybe? He was in command and knew it, not quite a swagger, more of a competence in every move he made.

I assumed I was done. The jogger that had waited with me was gone, the others dispersed as I talked with John. Turning back the way I had come I headed home, my walk spoiled by the gruesome find.

I was chilled through from standing in the breeze off the water, my sneakers damp from the wet sand. I wanted coffee, and lots of it.

I picked up the pace.

When I was home I changed my jeans as well as my socks and shoes. The cuffs were damp and sandy. A marvel of the beach is the amount of sand that follows you home no matter how careful you are. There will always be sand.

Seeing the time, I changed my mind, picked up my keys and headed for Kelly's. On top of everything else, I was not going to cook.

~~~

Like most small towns the seniors gathered in the mornings to discuss the happenings of the world around them, share their opinions, and mostly to belong, to need to be somewhere for a reason.

Here that gathering place is Kelly's, the local diner.

Another bonus to small town life, there was always someone you knew, if you wanted company. The food was good and plentiful. Lunch leftovers often became supper, two meals for the price of one. The coffee was excellent, no charge for refills, a plus for the geriatric crowd.

It's a great place for any meal, or just coffee and pie.

Being later than my usual arrival time I was surprised to find Sharon still reading the paper in her customary booth, fourth on the left side.

Sharon owned and operated the real estate office next door. She referred to Kelly's as her branch office, since she was often found here, doing a crossword puzzle, or reading over contracts.

I sometimes wondered if she paid part of the rent on Kelly's just to reserve her place. The surname Kelly had led some to speculate she might have an even deeper interest in the place.

The diner advertised itself as the Home of the Bottomless Pot, referring to the coffee, although locals had a whole string of jokes about the title.

A bell rang when the front door opened, alerting one and all that someone had arrived. Beside the front door was a cabinet on which resided trays of inverted coffee cups, all shapes, sizes, and colors, no two alike.

On entry, one grabbed the cup of their choice, carried it to their stool or booth and set it upright as a sign they were ready for coffee.

26

Tourists were easy to spot. They were the ones who sat, waited for their waitress, and then made the trip back to the front door to secure a cup. Our senior citizenry often noted the trip with a friendly elbow to the guy sitting next to him.

I snagged a purple cup of dubious ancestry that I had formed a kind of attachment to and made my way to Sharon's booth.

"You okay?" She said by way of greeting.

"Why?" I asked, setting my cup on the table so Sally, the waitress, could fill it on her next pass.

"The body," said Sharon. "Not something you do every day. I know it would put me off my feed." She looked at me from under her bangs, going through her shaggy dog faze of hair style, trying to let the bangs grow out.

"How did you know?"

"Really?" She waved her arm, indicating the counter and booths around us. "They knew before the cops got there. Who was it? Anyone we know?"

Of course she knew. Small town. I was surprised she didn't know who it was already.

Sally wandered up and filled my cup, taking out her order pad.

"Breakfast today, Tee?"

"Just coffee, Sally."

"Sure thing, hon," she scribbled on her pad. "Did you recognize the body?" she asked. "Was it Mildred's husband?"

"I don't know," I said. "I never really saw any details, just a big lump." A vision of the dark mass in the sand flitted across my mind. "I don't even know if it was a man or a woman, just a bundle of wet, dark clothes. No recognizable face." I shivered at the memory of the sand filled, empty eye sockets.

Sally sighed, and tucked her pencil behind her ear. "I hate to say it but I hope it is him. She's had a devil of a time with the insurance company, the police, everything, since the Coast Guard can't find anything."

She gave a swipe to the table and left.

"Who's Mildred?" I asked, reaching for the creamer and stirring some into my coffee.

"Where've you been?" said Sharon. "She's the vet's wife. You know, the vet that was lost at sea? Maybe three, four months back? You'd recognize her if you saw her. She's lived here most of her life."

I gave her a blank look.

Between chemo brain and brain radiation my memory was not what it once was. A good day was one where I didn't have to pull over to the curb and figure out where I was going, or exactly where it was.

"You don't remember?"

I shook my head and sipped coffee.

"The vet, Hammond. Dr. Vince Hammond. He went out fishing one day and never came back. They haven't found him or the guy who was with him. Can't even find the boat. It was a decent sized boat, ocean going, and not a sign of it, not even a board. Mildred is his wife."

Sally topped off our cups.

"That poor woman," she said, shaking her head. "I feel so bad for her. She can't get any answers from the Coast Guard. The cops can't help, although she gets to spend time with La Kincaid." She waggled her eyebrows. "She's selling her house to keep from losing it to foreclosure, going to move back east with her sister. Terrible thing. Can't settle the insurance without a body, just a mess."

A guy at the counter called to her and she picked up the coffee pot and left.

Sharon shrugged. "There, now you know. Do you think it was him?"

"No idea. I don't know if it was even a man." The memory of the bundle rolling around in the surf, slowly lifting and sliding forward, then back, pushed by the waves until it was grounded.

I hoped that memory would soon slide into the mental mist of my mind. I shivered again and reached for my coffee.

"Did you get to any sales today?" Sharon asked, sipping from her own cup.

"Not yet, and now it's kind of late. With all the stuff from this morning, my heart's not in yard sales. Besides, I still have some books from last week to go through. And I want to swing by Andy's and check on some glass ware." I pulled a crumpled five from my pocket and stuck it under the edge of my cup. "Enough to keep me busy."

Sharon stuck some folded bills under her plate and stood up, reaching over to give me a hug. "Good day for a nap," she grinned. To her, every day is a good day for a nap. As the owner of the real estate office next door she often went home to nap during the day, leaving a sign on the door.

"I have to get something done," I told her. "Can't waste the whole day."

She was the one who stuck with me during my cancer treatments, had several times driven me home from the hospital. Sharon made me her personal project for a while and I was grateful. She was also the one who suggested yard sales for book inventory and the one who pushed me to the Gem, back into living.

"I'm okay," I reassured her with a return hug. We walked out together, still chatting about nothing in particular.

Above us the gulls circled, filling the air with their lonely cries.

~~~

The following week I found myself wondering about the body, wondering if it had been identified, if Mildred had been reunited with her long lost husband.

A brief story in the paper only reported the bare facts, giving my name as the reporting person. An autopsy was scheduled, the results expected in a few weeks.

Every time I saw John across the drive, getting in or out of his truck, I thought about going over and asking him for an update. Then I'd decide against it and settle for checking the paper and watching the local news. My usual source, Sharon, had no more information than I did. Even the seniors at Kelly's had moved on to other topics.

The weekend's sales yielded little, giving me some needed time to work in the flower beds and trim the hedge that separated Miss Ellie from John.

I dragged out the hedge trimmer, garden shears and trash bags, and carried them to the driveway.

I noticed John's truck was gone and decided to start there, since he was gone and the noise wouldn't bother him.

I fired up the trimmer and started trimming the top first, moving down the length of the hedge to keep the top even. Working my way back I concentrated on the side, holding the trimmer at a slight angle so that the top was a little wider than the bottom.

The noise drowned out other sounds, so when someone tapped me on the shoulder I jumped a foot and dropped the trimmer, which cut a swath along the bottom of the hedge before the motor cut off.

"Sorry," said John, not looking sorry at all, "I didn't mean to scare you. If you'll let me use the trimmer I can do my own hedge."

"That's okay, it's my job," I said, picking up the trimmer. "I'm sorry. I didn't see your truck so I thought you were gone. Hope I didn't disturb you."

"Running late last night. I had my partner drop me off. My truck is still at the station. As a matter of fact I was going to ask if you could run me over to pick it up."

I stood there, looking at the trimmed twigs and leaves that needed to be raked up and bagged, and my supplies strewn around the yard. I finally looked up at him. "Sure. Can it wait till I just get this mess cleaned up? If I leave it right now it's going to get blown all over the place."

"Tell you what," he grinned, "how about I finish this? It's the least I can do." He picked up the rake and the roll of trash bags, tearing one off while he was speaking.

"I'll get my keys," I said.

By the time I had washed my hands, taken the time to brush the twigs and leaves from my hair, and grabbed my keys he had lined up three trash bags along the drive. The trimmer, shears and roll of bags sat by the garage door.

"I still have to do the other side," I said, "but thanks for the help."

He gave me a measuring look, like he had never seen me before, although he had lived forty feet away for over a year.

"It's my yard," he said. "I'll finish it when I get home from work. I've been meaning to ask if I could borrow the mower and tools. I like being outside."

I never heard of a tenant that wanted to do their own yard work. Ellie, my retired teacher, liked to plant her own flowers so I left that to her, while I did the lawn and the hedges. Her back yard was mostly garden so that, too, I left alone.

Hey, if he wanted to do it, great. Less for me to do.

"All yours," I said. "You ready?"

"Let me grab my jacket," he said, already moving across the lawn.

I got in my truck, backed out, and waited for him in the drive.

Like most people in town I knew where the police station was even though I had never been there. Once he was in and belted up I headed that way.

"Have you heard any more about the body?" I asked as we drove toward the center of town.

He glanced over at me, his eyes hidden behind sun glasses. He seemed to be deciding on an answer.

"It's the guy who owned the boat," he said finally.

"The vet?"

"Sorry, no. It was the other guy, Winnie, the one who owned the boat. Winnie took guys out fishing, made a few bucks on the side. Did you know Vince Hammond?"

"No, not really. I just heard the gang at Kelly's talking about him. Guess his wife is having a tough time."

"Death is never easy," he said, "no matter what the circumstances."

I thought about the cancer patients I had known, those treated right alongside me that did not make it.

All survivors carry a little sack of guilt around, wondering why we made it and others didn't. Celebrities like Farrah Fawcett and Patrick Swayze, beautiful people with so much talent, died too soon. Legendary tough guys John Wayne and Steve McQueen gone while I was allowed to live.

That ended my questions for the day.

When we reached the station he directed me around to the back of the building, to a parking lot surrounded by a chain link fence. I assumed these were personal vehicles. His silver pickup was near the gate, so I just pulled in behind it and stopped to let him out.

"Thanks for the lift. I appreciate it," he said as he stepped out.

"Thanks for raking up my mess," I answered and put the truck in reverse. "Have a nice day."

"You too," he nodded.

The longest conversation we ever had ended on that note.

I backed out and headed home.

I finished up the yard, bagged up the trimmings, and hauled the bags out to the curb to add to the row John had started, waiting for pickup tomorrow morning.

It was late afternoon by the time the tools were cleaned and put away. Time for a hot shower, sweats and something stuck between two pieces of bread and called supper.

I watched a television show I had recorded and half a movie before calling it a night. I was settling in with my Kindle and the cats when the familiar blue flash lit my mind.

FLASH

Hey Muse.

Hey, Tim.

What's going on? Haven't talked to you this week. Anything new? Find any great treasures?

Not lately. Found a body.

A body? A real body?

Well, yeah, what other kind of body is there?

I'll let that one go. Was it someone local? Someone you knew?

A missing fisherman. Two of them drowned, or at least disappeared, last spring. I found one of them.

Where was he?

In the shallows, washing in with the tide. Rolled him to the beach and grounded him there.

Creepy. Although someone somewhere is happy he's found.

Sad story, all the way around. The one still missing is the local vet. His wife can't settle his insurance. Sharon says she's going to have to sell their house. Behind on the payments. Can't keep the practice. The house, utilities, and all the other stuff is draining her.

Why? Vets are doctors. Animal doctors. I would think he had bucks.

I'm just going by what I hear.

Seems like the insurance company could work with her, give her some kind of advance.

You would think so. I mean, what if the body never washes in? That happens sometimes. Will she have to wait seven years, or whatever it is?

Guess that would depend on the policy. Do you know her? Personally I mean.

Nope, never met her. Didn't even know him. Several churches have helped, the bank even organized a fund raiser. No income, bills to be paid, gas, food, all the normal stuff that has to be paid, has to be tough.

Death is never easy.

You're the second guy to say that today.

Who was the first?

The cop on the case. He's the one who lives across from me. I gave him a lift to his truck.

He should be able to give you the inside info, if it's his case.

He seemed a little reluctant so I let it go. I don't really know him that well.

He's a tenant, you should know him. You should know everyone that lives close.

I know the basics. I try not to get involved with the tenants on a personal level. That could make for awkward situations. You know? Like they're going to be late on the rent, or something, and want a favor. I think it's best to keep some distance.

Still, it's nice to have a cop right at hand.

That it is.

Well, keep me up to date. Have a good night. Catch you later.

Night, Tim.

I picked up my Kindle and opened it to my current book.

Chapter Three

It was later in the week before a short article appeared on page six of the local paper, reporting the body had been identified as Winston 'Winnie' Sloan, the skipper on the lost fishing boat.

According to the article he had been single, a retired fisherman, who supplemented his retirement with small charters on his boat. His wife had preceded him in death and no other relatives had come forward. The autopsy was still in the works to determine a cause of death, with results still expected in a couple of weeks.

I wondered how CSI could get the results during a commercial break.

Like many news reports it rehashed the known facts - the boat reported overdue and missing, with two men believed to be on board. While Winston Sloan had no family, the veterinarian, Vincent Hammond, was survived by his wife, Mildred Hammond.

A rather gruesome footnote to the article asked all those on the beach to keep a sharp eye for anything unusual washing up. I hoped they meant boards.

I met with Sharon for lunch. Our Friday ritual was lunch and newspapers. She did the crossword puzzle while I read over the ads for the coming sales this weekend.

Today I had other things on my mind. I shoved my folded newspaper to the side as soon as we ordered.

"What do you know about the vet's wife?"

"Mildred?"

"Yeah. They identified the body I found, said it was the guy fishing with her husband. Still nothing new on the husband. Will that help her?"

"Beats me. I'm selling her house for her. I do know she's having a big yard sale this weekend." She sipped tea. "I called and left a message for you. Don't know what she's selling, may just be junk. Her house is already in escrow, for a quick sale, and she's trying to get things cleaned out so she can move. She says the insurance company is ready to settle, or close to it. It's only twenty thousand dollars, so they have no problem paying off. She wants to get on with it."

"If the insurance is going to settle, why sell the house? Although that's not a lot of money."

"She wants a new start, I guess. Can't fault her for that."

"Where's she going to move?" I asked, adding cream to my coffee.

"Not sure. I think she said East Coast, but who knows? You know how it is around here. You hear bits and pieces and then can't remember who you heard it from. I did ask her if she was having the yard sale this weekend and she said yes. She also said there were some larger pieces she was selling so she wouldn't have to move them."

Sally sauntered over and joined us. "You girls want menus? The special is fish and chips." She used the eraser end of the pencil to scratch her head. We knew the specials as well as she did after all these years.

They remained the same - Monday was pot roast, Tuesday was ham steak, Wednesday was macaroni and cheese, Thursday was chicken and dumplings and Friday was fish. The only options were Saturday and Sunday when it was chef's choice.

This being Friday I ordered the fish and chips, knowing there was no way I could eat it all. The leftovers warmed up nicely and relieved me of cooking supper. Not the act of a crazy person, right?

We chatted until Sally brought our meals.

"Sally, how well do you know the vet's wife?" I asked, making room for my salad.

"Mildred? Oh, I don't know. They lived across the street from my sister, so I know her to wave at if I see her. You know, chat about the weather, that kind of thing. My sis said the house sold on some kind of quick sale. You should know," she said to Sharon, poking her in the shoulder. "Didn't you handle the sale?"

"Sure did."

"The thing I don't understand," Sally said, continuing the conversation, "is how they didn't have any money. That's a nice house and that's a pricey neighborhood. My brother in law is a doctor on staff at the hospital. If the Hammonds could afford to live there they must have had some money. He was a vet. That's a doctor isn't it? "

She moved on, not waiting for us to agree or disagree.

I looked at Sharon. "Shouldn't they have money?"

Sharon shrugged. "I would think so. We only have two vets in town and he's been here the longest. The other vet is a large animal vet, works mostly with cattle and horses."

She grinned suddenly and leaned closer.

"Could be a plot," she said, lowering her voice. "Word around town was that his business was going downhill. He was not the most popular guy in town. The new vet in San Luis was already getting a lot of his customers. You read all those mysteries. Doesn't that sound suspicious?"

"That he was losing his patients? In that case, he should have killed the other vet."

We sipped coffee.

"Mildred spent the last year or so working in his office. He let his other help all go," Sharon continued. "For a while they were living in high cotton. Vacations in Europe, went to Hawaii several times. I heard they were going to Vegas once a month or so. That would take some bucks."

"I would think so."

Sharon leaned back again. "I've also heard he got kind of gruff the last year, with his patients and their owners. No wonder he was losing his clients. You know how people are. Their pets are like their kids. Get rough with one and they won't come back."

"Sounds like the wife may be better off without him," I said, then felt badly. "Sorry, that was out of line."

With a wave of her hand Sharon brushed it aside. "From all I've heard they had a good marriage, seemed to be happy. I've talked to her some the last few weeks, getting the paperwork done for the sale of the house. She seems to be resigned now, looking forward to getting away, starting over. She's moving back east to be with her sister. She's a looker, and with the insurance money and the money from the house, she won't be lonesome long."

"It's sad enough to lose your husband, then have to leave your home." I knew about losing your home from experience. Mine had gone to short sale so I didn't lose it.

40

The money had gone to medical bills. "I hope she gets a new start."

"And be sure to check her yard sale. Might be something good there." She tossed her napkin onto the table and pulled out her wallet, waving to Sally to bring the check. "My treat today."

Sally brought the check and took Sharon's credit card. I pulled out some bills and left the tip.

"Where does your sister live," I asked Sally when she brought the charge slip for Sharon to sign.

"Over on Maple, middle of the 1500 block. Why?"

I grinned at her. "Yard sale."

Sally shook her head, slipped the tip in her pocket, and wandered off with the credit slip.

~~~

Saturday dawned bright and clear, always a good sign for outdoor sales. Beach towns often have overcast, damp mornings from either fog or the marine layer thick overhead. Those bright sunny days shown on television are not that common, and usually mean the wind is blowing. Early sun always cheered me.

I showered, dressed in jeans and sweat shirt, pulled on some boots and gathered my things. I use my phone for almost everything so it goes in my pocket, with my cash. My digital camera, notebook, pens, odds and ends get jammed in a fanny pack so my hands are free.

I filled a travel cup and thermos with coffee and headed out, my newspaper already marked. Across the top of the page I had written Mildred's name, so I wouldn't forget to swing by her sale, to see what she had. I wanted to help her out if I could.

When you've been down due to circumstances you can't control, you appreciate what others are going through a lot more. Besides, if everyone was right, they should have some nice things. He was by general consensus a type of doctor.

Cruising the first few sales, there was nothing that really caught my interest, mostly clothes just jumbled into piles, no effort put into appearances. Some people seem to just throw stuff out the front door onto the grass and wait for people to hand them money while others take the time to sort, price and display, even adding balloons or clever signs to their wares.

One of my favorite signs: "Lying, cheating jerk's stuff for sale. Cheap" Another read "Parachute for sale. Used once, never opened. Small stain."

Speaking from my personal experience, those who took the extra time, whether balloons, signs or just nice displays, were my favorites. These are where you find the good stuff. People who take the time for their sales take care of their stuff.

First stop netted two beautiful pieces of Lalique glass for fifty cents. Andy would love these, guaranteed to be a profit for both of us. Also a nice Carnival glass pitcher that I could use if Andy didn't want it.

For a dollar, you can't beat it.

When I first started buying from these sellers I felt obligated to tell them they were underpricing their items. I learned that few appreciate you informing them they're mistaken, especially the seniors, that they have no idea what they're doing. In the case of our seniors, I added a few extra bucks to the asking price or bought something I didn't want to try to balance it out.

I kept my own box of those things to take to the thrift store.

The morning was passing and I didn't have much to show. The last five yard/garage sales were duds. One lady was selling empty mayonnaise jars for a dollar. Another sold used cloth diapers three for five dollars.

I didn't even know if anyone used cloth diapers any more. Unless you needed a good dust cloth.

The coffee I had brought along was cold.

Swinging by the fast food drive-thru I refilled my coffee cup. Fortified with fresh caffeine I pulled into a parking slot and turned off the truck. Sipping coffee, I checked my newspaper, marking off the sales I had seen already, making sure I hadn't missed any.

FLASH

Hey, Muse.

Hey, yourself Tim. What are you doing here this time of day?

Did I violate a rule?

No, of course not. It's just that you usually show up at night.

I just wondered what you were up to today. Big plans?

You know I never have big plans. Just hitting the yard sales.

Anything good?

Yep, already made some money. Coffee break right now.

How was the sale at the widow's house?

Next stop. I wanted to hit these others early.

Maybe she'll have some good things for you. Cleaning out a house is a big job, even bigger if you lived there for a while. I imagine she'll be getting rid of his stuff, too.

You never know. Some wives want to keep their husbands things.

Guess it depends on the things.

And the husband.

You may have a point there. From what you told me, this may depend on space available too. Didn't you say she was moving out of state?

I think that's what I heard. Arizona? East Coast? Moving to be near her sister, I think. She doesn't have any family around here.

Well, then she really has to pare it down to basics. Movers get a pretty penny, even more if it's clear across the country.

I really would like to help her out. Just don't know if she has anything I can use.

Old underwear and girdles?

Very funny, Tim. The lady is a looker. I doubt she owns a girdle. With any kind of luck there might be some good books.

Ok, get to work. I'll check back later to see how it went. Are my times limited now? Only at night?

Of course not. I was just surprised to hear you this early.

Then I'll talk to you soon.

Okay

Tim does have his drawbacks. He usually says bye when he goes but there have been a few times when I thought he was gone and he says something.

He's my afterthought I guess. I am so accustomed to him that I don't think about it, although him showing up during the day could be a definite drawback, if I was, for instance, blazing down the freeway in traffic.

I don't even know how long he's been around, he's just there, like my other self, the one with common sense whose memory didn't fail at inconvenient times. For whatever reason, he shows up when he feels like it and I am always glad to hear him.

I said before, he is the ultimate companion. I never worry when he's sick. I don't even know if he gets sick. He never hogs the covers or leaves the toilet seat up, and never complains about dinner or lack thereof. Always asks about my day and listens to my answer. Hard to beat that combination, even with a figment of your own imagination.

I started the truck and headed for Mildred's.

~~~

There were already cars at her house, parked up and down the block on both sides of the street. People were milling around the tables and driveway, the larger pieces to the rear, closer to the house. Easier to put back if they didn't sell, plus a backdrop for the smaller items.

I found a place to park the truck about half a block away and stowed my coffee.

Walking back I noticed the people leaving were carrying things, some by the bag full, which is a good sign of reasonable prices.

There is something about stepping into a yard, the smell of the grass, the scent of someone's coffee riding the air, the guilty pleasure of someone else's treasures spread before you like the great open air markets of the Middle East. There's a lot on view about the person behind the table, stories in the scales people shed from their lives at these sales.

What child held these children's classics, and who read them to eager, bright eyed kids wiggling in their beds for the bedtime story? What occasioned the limp and faded gowns to be tossed on a tarp beside used plastic containers? Which child would miss the doll or bunny laying on a blanket?

Stepping onto the lawn I saw Mildred sitting at a small table with a money box. Seeing her in person, I placed her. Although we had never met, I have seen her around town, in stores, the gas station, that kind of thing.

She had a clipboard and several pencils spread in front of her. She was wearing a bright yellow visor and a hot pink sweatshirt emblazoned with a Nike swoosh. She was about my age, with great hair. Being bald for over a year makes me extremely conscious of other people's hair. Mine is long enough now that I can go out without people staring but not really long enough to style.

I was so accustomed to the ease of wash and go hair that I was pretty sure I was going to keep it this short. I could admire lovely styles while being content with my pixie locks.

"Hi, Mildred, how's it going," I greeted her. "Looks like a good turnout this morning."

"Oh, hi. Tee, isn't it? Lots of little things, not much on the bigger stuff. Still, it is money and that's the whole

46

point." She smiled up at me and I could see the circles under her eyes that makeup did not quite cover completely. With all she had been through these past months it was understandable.

"We haven't officially met, but I did want to extend my sympathies. I hope you do really well with your sale."

She reached to pat my hand. "Thank you, dear. Everyone has been so kind. Did you know Vincent?"

"No, ma'am, I'm sorry, I never met him. I don't have much call to see a veterinarian."

I didn't want to tell her that a lot of people didn't see his disappearance as a big loss. From some of the rumors I heard, he wasn't popular and his business was failing, not something you wanted to share with the grieving widow.

"Well, I'm going to wander around, see what I can find," I said, moving away from the table.

"Oh, go ahead! There must be something here you can't live without. I've seen you at the library. I put the books over there," she indicated the general direction of the porch. "So they won't have to move them too far when it's over."

"Good idea. Do you need help? I can come back by and give you a hand."

"Oh, no, no, I was smart enough to hire the boys next door. They helped bring things out, and they'll be back to help put it away. What doesn't sell I'm just going to put in the garage or on the porch and have the thrift store come pick up. I don't want it all put back in the house."

"That's thinking ahead," I agreed. "If you need help here's my number," I slid one of my cards across the table to her.

"Thank you so much, I appreciate it, I really do." She opened her cash box and tucked the card inside. "Now, go look around. There has to be something to pique your interest. All prices are negotiable," she smiled and gave me a wink.

I smiled back and wandered away to scout out the scene.

Larger items were lined up to the rear of the yard, up close to the front porch and near the garage. Several dressers, small bookcases and bed tables or night stands made an irregular line along the walk from porch to garage. Behind them loomed the largest pieces, closest to the porch. One of these caught my eye.

The hall tree was old but well cared for during its lifetime, the finish deepened by years of waxing and rubbing by who knew how many hands. The stories it could tell if only inanimate things could speak or record their memories. How many homes in how many places had this piece held up coats and scarves and umbrellas? There is the wonder of antiques.

Rocking it back and forth gently said it was solid, a walk around it showed it had no scars or blemishes. I stepped back far enough to get a full length photo, took several from the front and sides, there being not enough room between it and the porch railing to get a good shot of the back.

Moving to the end of the row gave me an angled shot across the back, enough to show no damages or marks, so I took a couple more shots, adding a last one of the side facing me, to capture the gleam of its fine finish in the morning sun.

I grouped the shots in an email with my phone and sent them to Andy, pretty sure this would be of interest. Wandering back to Mildred at her table I asked the price, turning to admire the hall tree where it stood guard at the edge of the porch. I snapped off a couple of more pictures now that the sun had lit it to a lustrous, glowing gem against the backdrop of the gray house. My phone takes good pictures, the digital camera takes great pictures that can be enlarged if need be to show more detail. I pulled my camera out of my fanny pack and took a few more pictures with it.

"How much for the hall tree?"

Mildred had been watching me snap pictures of the furniture. She looked first at me, then back toward the house where the hall tree gleamed in the sunlight.

"Two hundred? I've had it for years. My mother gave it to me and I never really liked it. You know how it is when your mother gives you something. She checks for the rest of your life to see if you're taking care of it." She looked back at me. "It's funny, once she passed on, I never even noticed it, just shoved it in the spare room and left it. I don't know its history, or even where she got it."

"Let me check with someone. Can you hold it for maybe ten, fifteen minutes?"

She looked back at the hall tree, a small frown line forming between her brows. "Well, I guess so, I mean, unless someone else has the cash. I don't mean to be rude, Tee, but I'm trying to sell this stuff and move on. You understand," she smiled.

"Good enough. I'm only going to make a phone call, I'll be right over there," I pointed to my truck.

"That's fine," she mumbled, her gaze already wandering back toward the house where two women were going through the boxes of books.

I speed dialed Andy while walking back to the truck. Grabbing my thermos off the front seat I managed to pour a cup of coffee while balancing the phone between my shoulder and ear.

Andy answered before I got the lid back on the thermos.

"Hey, Andy, did you see the pics of the hall tree?"

"I was just looking at them," he said. "Did you get digital pics, too?"

"Sure did, knew you'd want them to load online."

"How much?"

"She wants two hundred, no provenance or anything."

"Hmmm, hang on just a sec," the phone clicked to hold and I sipped coffee. Minutes passed before Andy was back.

"You still there?"

"Oh, yeah. What's the verdict?"

"Sounds good. Bring it on over to the shop, and I'll cut you a check. Three okay?"

"Sounds great. See you in a few," I answered and clicked off. Fast hundred dollars for the day if nothing else sold. Tossing the cup back on the seat of the truck, I pulled my cash out of my pocket and counted off a hundred and five twenties. I keep three hundred in cash on hand for just such purchases, although this was my first purchase of over a hundred.

Making my way back over to Mildred, I handed her the folded over bills. "There you go, for the hall tree.

Okay if I leave it there till I look through the other stuff?"
I took the time to put my camera back into the fanny pack.

"Of course, dear! Thank you so much," she tucked the
bills into her pocket. "Anything else, just ask. Will you
need help loading that thing?"

"Not sure, let me look around first to see if there's
anything else."

I wandered back around the yard, looking in the boxes.
Several boxes of books looked interesting but I didn't
want to take the time to check every book.

"How much for the books?" I called to her.

"One dollar each, or ten dollars a dozen."

"How about both boxes? Can you give me a break if I
take them all?"

I watched her duck her head and do some scribbling
on her clip board. "How about thirty for both boxes?"

I didn't think they were worth that much but I did want
to help her. A shoe box of costume jewelry caught my eye
as I straightened up. The box was marked five bucks, so I
sat it on top of the first box of books and picked up the
whole thing to carry out to the truck.

Stopping at her table I showed her the box of jewelry
atop the books.

"I want the other box, too, so that's thirty five for all of
it?"

She reached out to pat my hand.

"Thirty is fine for all of it, and thank you," she smiled.

I unzipped the fanny pack and pulled out my wallet,
handing her a twenty and a ten. This was the end of my
shopping for today, at least until I got the check from
Andy.

"Do you need a receipt?" she asked.

"Yes, ma'am, I do," I answered. "I'm going to load this box, then I'll get the other box and the hall tree."

She reached for her book of receipts while I picked up the box of books and headed to the truck.

I opened the gate on the Explorer, slid the box of books in beside another box I had forgotten was there, and realized there is no way the hall tree was going to fit.

Calling Andy came up blank, just his voice mail, meaning he was either out or ignoring his calls. I left a message to call me back, slammed the gate shut and hiked back up the block.

Several people were grouped around Mildred's table. I waited my turn, trying Andy one more time, shifting from foot to foot, watching the time creep past.

"Yes? Is there something else?"

"Oh, sorry, Mildred," I apologized, "is it okay if I leave the hall tree for a little bit? It's not going to fit in my truck. I have a friend with a pickup I can borrow, it's just going to take a little while."

She lifted one hand over her eyes like a visor and looked up at me.

"Well, for how long? I can't have it sitting there all night."

"Oh, no, no, not that long, maybe two hours?"

"I guess that will be all right, just not much longer. I have people coming to pick up the things that don't sell. I don't want to have to start separating them."

"I'll get it just as quick as I can," I said, thinking to myself, you have the money so what do you care? And what happened to anything you need?

I grabbed the other box of books and lugged it back down the street, slinging it in the truck. Andy still wasn't answering the phone so I left him a message to call me right away, hopped in the truck and drove home.

I had all the boxes out of the truck and into the house by the time Andy finally got back to me. He was on a delivery run, thirty miles out of town, not sure how soon he would get back. I debated calling Mildred to tell her I was running late, then realized I didn't have her number.

I nuked some leftover coffee, cooled it down with milk, and sipped the bitter brew while my mind spun around trying to grab traction. Standing over the sink I was looking out the kitchen window.

Right at John's pretty silver pickup truck.

Pouring out the coffee, I went out the side door, across the yard and knocked on his door.

After a few minutes, I knocked again, a little louder. I didn't hear anything and was backing away from the door when it suddenly popped open, making me jump.

John stood there, his brown eyes cold as stone, holding a towel. His chest was bare, wide and muscled, stacked over hips which were fortunately covered in jeans.

I felt my cheeks getting red, the flush crawling up from my neck. His hair was wet enough to still be dripping on one side. He swiped at it with the towel, still looking at me with that icy stare.

"Hi. Sorry to bother you," I stammered, looking away from the expanse of his chest, knowing my face was red. "I was wondering if I could borrow your truck. I bought a piece of furniture at a yard sale and it won't fit in my Explorer. It's just the other side of town, won't take long," I realized I was babbling.

He tossed the towel to the side.

"No" he said.

After a really uncomfortable minute, he sighed. "Let me grab a shirt and some shoes and I'll take you where you need to go."

I already regretted this bright idea but could see no graceful exit.

"Oh, okay, although I am a good driver. I really hate to inconvenience you," I said to his bare back as he stepped out of sight.

"No problem," he called from somewhere inside.

I stood there, not sure if I should follow him, or wait outside.

He made the decision for me, stepping back outside, and closing the door behind him. He had pulled on a sweatshirt and slip on canvas shoes. His keys jingled in his hand. "Let's go."

I followed him over to the truck where he opened the passenger door for me, stepped back and waited for me to climb in. I had to squeeze by him to get in the front seat, acutely aware of how good he smelled, and felt my face flame again. I caught a glimpse of a small smile as he carefully shut my door and walked around to the other side.

"Where to?" He clipped his seat belt, glanced over to be sure mine was secure and started the engine.

"It's on Maple, do you know where that is?"

"I'm a cop. I know everything," he actually grinned and backed down the drive.

"Good to know," I mumbled.

He drove well, both hands on the wheel, checking traffic at every intersection. As his hair dried, it curled slightly, the ends glinting gold in the sunlight coming in his window. I pulled my eyes back to the front, my cheeks still feeling warm.

"Left or right?"

I had mentally wandered off again. Oops. I hoped it was yet another reminder of those months of chemo. "Left," I said, pointing to the right. "I mean, right, sorry." I felt the blush again, knowing he must think I'm an idiot. Sadly, I couldn't blame the chemo. This was on me, not focusing.

He quickly corrected the truck and turned to the right.

"Right up there, by those cars. Anywhere along here will be fine."

He pulled to an open space at the curb and turned off the truck. Mildred's yard was still a couple of houses up.

"The Hammond place?" he asked.

"Yes. You know it?"

"Yeah, I was here quite a bit, when he was first reported missing. I had to talk to Millie quite a few times." John glanced at me, opened his door and climbed down from the truck. I opened the door quickly and got to the sidewalk before he did, still wishing I had passed on this bright idea.

He met me on the sidewalk and we turned together towards Mildred's yard.

"I like this neighborhood. I'd like to live here," he said, looking around at the different homes.

"Are you giving me notice?"

"Oh, no. Not yet anyway. Just something to file away for the future. Some day. I like the look of it. Like an old magazine cover."

I smiled at him. "Norman Rockwell syndrome?"

He chuckled. "Exactly! You remember those? A lot of people have never heard of him," he grinned approvingly, a very attractive grin. "My dad had a book of his prints, and collected the old Post magazines. I spent a lot of rainy afternoons going through those magazines."

"Does your dad live around here?" I asked.

"Over in the valley, about a three hour drive."

"How did you get into police work?"

"Natural progression. Military MP. Deputy Sheriff."

"Here in the county?"

"Nope, in Los Angeles. I was there for several years."

"You must have seen a lot. Did you have any interesting cases?"

"They're all interesting, one way or another. You see some of the worst people in the world, and some of the best. It's never boring. Lots more paperwork than people think, and so much of it is detail. Contrary to movies and television most criminals are not that bright."

"I would think the big city would be more exciting than Monarch Beach."

He paused for a second and gave me a shuttered look, the coldness returning to his eyes. Not quite as friendly. "I like a small town better."

I felt like he had slammed a door in my face.

We had reached Mildred's yard. I caught her eye and motioned to the back where the hall tree still stood. For just a minute she looked totally blank, then she nodded and gave me a weak smile. Several people were lined up in front of her table, money in hand, so I led the way to my treasure, anxious to get it loaded and get back home.

"This is it," I said.

John reached out and tilted the hall tree. "Not too heavy, seems pretty solid." He walked around to the other side, leaning to check the back. "It is a pretty piece of work."

"You know antiques?"

He glanced at me. "Like the guy said, I know what I like, and I like this. Nice piece of furniture."

Good taste, I thought, and added it to his resume. "I think we can just carry it down to the curb and load it up."

"Sounds good," he said, reaching up to catch the top rail and beginning to tip it over. "Get this end. I'll get the bottom."

Not being one to argue, I stepped over and caught the top.

"Got it?"

"Yep, I'm good."

He went back and caught the bottom rail, lifting it to a horizontal position, and began backing towards the street.

When we reached the curb, he sat the heavier end down on the grass verge beside the street.

"Can you hold it while I run get the truck?
"I've got it. If it gets too much I'll set it down."

He turned and trotted back to his truck with the easy gait of a runner. Within minutes he pulled up at the curb, headed the wrong way, on the wrong side of the street.

"Just a minute," he called, and strode across the lawn toward Mildred and her table. I looked around to see what he was doing. He was bent at the waist, holding out some bills to Mildred.

My end was getting heavier by the minute, so I eased it to the grass. Glancing up I saw John nodding and smiling with Millie, warm and friendly. She smiled back radiantly, none of the weak attempts I got. She chuckled at something he said, reached to take the money and gave his arm a couple of pats. From where I stood, along the curb, it looked like she was flirting with him.

I remembered his earlier remark, about being in the neighborhood recently. Of course he would be here. He was investigating her husband's disappearance. He would also know Mildred, from those interviews.

With a pat on her shoulder and another smile John picked up a bundle by the table and trotted back to the truck.

He held up a blanket and shook it out. "Keep it from getting scratched up in the truck bed," he said, spreading the blanket across the bed of the truck.

"Ready?" He glanced my way and I nodded.

Between us we lifted the hall tree and slid it up into the truck. John grabbed a side rail and pulled himself up into the bed where he could maneuver the heavier base up close to the cab, bunching up some blanket as a cushion. When he got it where he wanted, he hopped over the side and came around to fasten the tailgate. Good thing he had the extended bed. The hall tree was flush to the gate.

"All set," he said. "Back to the house?"

"That would be great."

In just minutes we were back at the house, the hall tree unloaded and gracing my porch, waiting for Andy to pick it up.

I pulled a ten out of my pocket and extended it. "Thank you so much. You really saved me."

He glanced at the bill in my hand, then brought his gaze back up to me. He seemed to be measuring me, the dark eyes glinting. I was beginning to fidget, dropping the hand holding out the money.

"Tell you what. How about you fix me dinner one night and we call it even." His gaze was steady now, holding me.

"I can manage that I think," I answered. "You pick a night."

"Tomorrow too soon? I'm off tomorrow night."

"You have a deal," I said and stuck out my hand. He regarded my outstretched hand for a minute or two, finally taking it and giving it a light shake before quickly dropping it.

"Sounds good," he said." What time?"

"Six? Seven? Whatever's best for you?" I was having trouble meeting his eyes, looking at my shoes, the yard, anything but his direct gaze.

He thought for another minute. "Let's make it seven and I'll bring the wine," he finally said.

"Seven it is, and thanks again."

"See you tomorrow," he said, turning to climb back into his truck and backing across the drive into his own parking slot. He hopped out of the truck and walked to his steps, already talking on his cell phone.

I headed inside and called Andy again. This time he was there and agreed to swing by on the way home and pick up the hall tree. And drop off my check.

Chapter Four

I spent the following day online, researching, cataloging and loading titles from the assorted boxes I had brought home the day before. Although tedious, this is the best part, the treasure hunt, knowing that the very next book could be valuable. Of course, it still has to sell before I see a profit. Sometimes items sit for months, sometimes they sell the next hour.

Several times my mind wandered back to the odd exchange with John yesterday, wondering if he really would show up this evening. He had seemed so preoccupied when I first asked for his help, so unresponsive, that I was surprised he had agreed to help. And then he suggested having dinner with me? Odd, indeed.

The box of jewelry I left for last. The books were pretty standard, no real treasures, like the first edition To Kill a Mockingbird resting in my bedroom lawyer's bookcase, right next to a first edition Carrie. Those are my real treasures and I keep them out of sight although I doubt most people would recognize their true value.

Cancer often comes back. Those two books were my insurance that if I had to do it all over again, I could pay for my treatment.

The bottom of the box yielded a dozen map back paperbacks from the forties that were in pretty good shape, and listed from ten to thirty dollars apiece. I checked them all for mildew, smells, marks or stains and any identifying marks from previous owners. I fanned through each one. You would be really surprised at the things people stick between the pages.

I have found money, including a one hundred dollar bill, love letters, ticket stubs, an amazing variety of receipts, one for a bridal set of rings, dated 1941. I wondered at the time if this was a soldier, home on leave, headed for the front. Did she say yes? Since he had also purchased the wedding band, I think he was pretty sure of her answer.

I took pictures of every new item and transferred them to the appropriate file on the computer. Accurate records backed up my pathetic memory. After ten months of chemo, radiation and the additional two weeks of brain radiation, my memories bounced around like the numbered balls in a bingo game. Once proud of an excellent memory, I was now content to get through the day.

FLASH

Hey, Muse. How was the shopping today? Treasure?

Hey, Tim. Made a hundred from Andy. Bought a bunch of books and about half of them listed out. Still have a shoe box of junk jewelry to go through. I'm going to leave that for tomorrow. I'm tired.

I suddenly realized the time.

I stood up and stretched. I had company coming for dinner in just two hours.

Whoa, and I have a guest coming for dinner, so I better get cleaned up. Lost track of time.

Guest? Anyone I know?

John, the cop across the drive? He helped me load up a hall tree for Andy yesterday. I'm doing dinner as a thank you.

Your idea?

No, it was his idea.

Aha, romance rears its ugly head.

Having dinner is hardly a romance.

I don't know. He's been there for quite a while. Never invited himself over before.

He never helped me before.

Why didn't that dealer guy help?

Andy? He was out on a delivery.

And you couldn't wait?

What's with you tonight?

Just curious. Gotta be careful, Muse. He may have designs on you.

It's just dinner, Tim, and as late as it is, I'm going to have to buy it.

Okay, okay, just be careful. Talk to ya later.

~~~

I called my favorite chef at Tahlia's and ordered one of the house specialties to be picked up. I can cook, really, I just wanted something a little more special than my own cooking and time was running out. I put together a salad, covered it with waxed paper and stuck it in the fridge before heading for the shower.

Showered, legs shaved, and dressed in clean jeans and a sweater, I grabbed my keys and left to pick up dinner.

I couldn't help but be a little excited. First, that John was coming to dinner, and second, let's be honest, at what all the other single gals were going to think if they found out I was having dinner with the town's most eligible bachelor.

When I got to the restaurant I spent a few minutes visiting with Miguel, the chef, catching up on news of his kids. The smells were heavenly. I added a loaf of fresh bread, and two slices of tiramisu to the order and carried it all out to the truck. Heading back home I hoped John liked pasta. Of course, if he didn't, more for me.

I admit I was looking forward to dinner. It had been a long time since anyone other than Sharon had even stopped by.

While it was not a date exactly, it was a man coming to my house, a very good looking, and available man. On every level that made me feel good.

I put clean towels in the downstairs bathroom, picked up books from the coffee table in the living room, took out the trash, all the little things you do when someone new is coming to visit.

I set the table, checked that everything for dinner was ready, and loaded the coffee pot for after dinner coffee.

Flash.

Hey, Muse, how's it going?

Getting everything ready for dinner.

That's right, it's date night.

Not a date, Tim, just dinner.

So who is this guy?

He's the cop across the drive. He drops off his rent check and I wave at him when I see him. I've seen him at

*the Gem. Sharon knows him. He's the one who told her
about Mildred's husband.*

And he's coming for dinner because?

*As a thank you for helping me move the hall tree. I told
you that.*

He invited himself for dinner.

*It was mutual. I'm looking forward to sitting down to a
nice dinner and some conversation with someone I can
actually see.*

Whoa, testy. Okay, got it. Then I'll see you.

At exactly seven I saw John come out of his house
carrying flowers and a bottle of wine. Prompt. I like that.

I was at the door by the time he knocked.

Swinging the door wide, I motioned for him to come
in and closed the door behind him. He extended the
flowers and the bottle of wine.

"Thank you, John. I love fresh flowers," I said, taking
them and the wine.

"Have a seat." I carried the flowers to the kitchen,
pulled down a vase and filled it with water. Flower
arranging is not one of my virtues. I fluffed them out a
little and added them to the table.

Back in the living room, John had made Dave's
acquaintance. The cat sat on the arm of the couch with one
paw on John's shoulder, leaning forward, sniffing along
his neck.

"Dave, get down," I said firmly, giving him a gentle
shove.

"He's okay, really. I like cats. His name I take it is
Dave?'

"This one is Dave. There's two of them. His brother is Cletus. You won't see Cletus, he's the shy one. They're my aunt's cats. I just take care of them."

"Odd names for cats."

"James Lee Burke. My aunt loves all his books. They're named for characters in his books."

He looked up at me with a startled expression. "Dave Robicheaux and Cletus Purcell," he smiled. "I'm a fan."

I smiled back at him, glad to have a subject for discussion.

"So am I. She has all his books," I said, waving towards the bookcases beside the front door. "She isn't really an animal person. These two were abandoned, and abused pretty bad. They were here when she bought the property, almost dead, and she saved them. Not being an animal person, she named them after something familiar. Dave and Cletus. I've always been glad she wasn't reading Russian lit."

He chuckled. "I try to read every night before bed, helps me leave the job at work. I'd like to own a lot of books," he said, looking at the full bookcases. "Maybe one day. Right now, I try to get to the library once a week."

"If you need something to read, feel free," I said. "It's a genetic thing in my family. We all love books. I know my aunt has all the Burke novels, if you haven't read them all. You're certainly welcome to borrow one."

He gave me another of his odd measuring looks. "I may take you up on that," he said finally.

"I can always run you down if you don't return them."

"I guarantee I take care of my books. And I appreciate the offer. Believe me, I will take you up on it.

"Hungry?"

"Always," he said, standing.

"Right this, way," I said, gesturing to the table. I noticed he was reading titles as he passed the book cases on his way to the table.

We made small talk while we ate, mostly about books, the ones we most enjoyed, the ones we had been disappointed with, and recommending favorites to each other.

I got up to clear the table and make coffee. John followed me back to the kitchen, carrying our plates and the pasta bowl.

"Thanks," I said, taking them from him and rinsing them before stacking them in the sink.

"Thanks for dinner. It was delicious."

"I'd like to take the credit, but it was all from Tahlias."

"I'll make a note. I haven't been there. If this is any indication I'll be a regular."

"It's always good. Everything he makes is wonderful."

"Duly noted," he smiled.

We took our coffee back to the living room and I knelt to light the fireplace. Another nice thing about coastal living, the evenings are cool enough for a fire. Even in summer our weather will cool off by sunset.

"Tell me about your work," I said, once we were settled again.

I realized I had asked while John had a mouth full of coffee. I kept talking to avoid an awkward moment. "I noticed you talking to Mildred Hammond when we picked up the hall tree. Do you know her?"

He swallowed and sat back.

"Millie? I'm handling her case, or really, his case. The missing boat and the missing husband. I've interviewed her several times. So, in answer to the question, yes I know her, but not in a personal way, if that makes sense."

"Her case is closed then?"

"That one is still under investigation. That means I can't talk about it," he smiled to take the sting out of his words.

"Oh, I thought the case was closed once they found the body?"

He quirked an eyebrow at me, leaning forward to set his cup on the table.

"The body you found wasn't the husband. He's still missing. The body you found was the fisherman that owned the boat. There will have to be an autopsy, since he died under unknown circumstances. Then it's the medical evidence, forensics and all the scientific facts."

He lifted his cup and finished the coffee. "It's pretty much cut and dried when there's a life lost at sea. The victims don't always surface. There have been cases where they are never found. That's the basis for the seven years law, the law requiring a person to be missing for seven years to be declared legally dead. Depending on the policy and the insuring company, settlements can be made earlier. I'm not an expert on insurance law. We have to be careful with reports because of the insurance companies."

"Well, if Mildred is expecting her check, the insurance company must believe he's dead. Right?"

"We're not a hotbed of insurance fraud," he grinned.

I noticed how his eyes crinkled at the corners when he smiled.

"And the check wasn't that big, not for those guys," I said, pulling my gaze away as I gathered up the cups and plates and stacked them.

"Quarter million dollars isn't chicken feed," he said, picking up the dishes and heading for the kitchen.

"That's odd. I could swear she told me twenty thousand."

"You must have misunderstood. Its $250,000, according to the insurance agent. He's been in several times, checking to see what we've found, what the Coast Guard has found, that kind of thing."

"I thought I heard $20,000."

"I'm pretty sure the insurance investigator said quarter million."

"You're probably right. I have a terrible memory anymore."

"Someone told me you'd had cancer. That has to be tough, on anyone. You're in remission now?"

"At this particular moment in time, according to my tests, I am cancer free. Not the same as remission." "That's great news, isn't it?"

"I hope so. I still have to be tested, some tests at three months, some at six. If I get to three years, I have a good chance of beating it completely."

"Been pretty rough?"

"To tell you the truth it's not something I want to remember."

"Can't blame you. Glad you made it, though," he said with another of his rare smiles. "Otherwise I would have missed this dinner."

I laughed. "Ok, that was pretty lame."

He grinned and shrugged. "I tried. I'm out of practice. I really did enjoy dinner. And the company."

"You mean Dave?" Was I fishing for compliments? What the heck was wrong with me? I felt my cheeks warming up again.

He thought about it for a minute. "I meant you, although I enjoyed meeting Dave. Next time, I'll do dinner and you bring the wine."

"I can manage that," I said. "And I really can cook."

"I didn't doubt it for a minute," he said. "I've smelled some pretty good stuff cooking over here." He picked up his jacket from the chair where he'd tossed it when he came in. "I'll be happy to trade meals for furniture delivery any time."

He was standing at the door, jacket in hand.

I didn't know protocol so I just reached around him and opened the front door. He tipped up my chin and kissed my cheek.

"Thank you. We'll do it again. Soon." He stepped out the door, into the night, and headed across the lawn towards his house. Without turning around he waved over his shoulder, somehow sensing I was watching him.

I went back to the kitchen and loaded the dishwasher. It was nice to see the lights across the drive, to know more about the guy who lived there. I wondered if Aunt Johnnie had a rule about dating the tenants. I decided not to ask.

I hoped we would do it again. Soon.

~~~

The next day was breakfast for me and the cats then back to my desk to finish cataloguing books. Books always took longer than any other item, mostly because I rarely met a book I didn't like. Some called out to be read, or at least get a chance to tell their story, while others had been read, and enjoyed, and deserved a good home.

I browsed more than I loaded online.

There were several more good ones to add to the inventory, several more to add to the TBR, to be read, pile and a cookbook I thought Sharon might like. That was set aside, also.

There was only the jewelry left to do and that is so tedious I decided to put it off till after lunch. Standing and stretching I glanced across the drive. John's truck was gone. I never seemed to hear him come or go.

I made a peanut butter sandwich and ate it over the sink, along with a glass of milk. I rinsed the glass and set it to drain. I needed to get to the market, a chore I hated and put off till the last minute. Checking the cat's food I decided this was the time and grabbed my keys, headed out the door.

It was another bright, sunny day, the kind I had so enjoyed before I got sick. I was so passive during treatment, so weak and tired all the time. Now lethargy was a habit, one I had to fight. With the online business there was no real call to even get dressed, not like a real job. There were days I stayed in pajamas or sweats all day.

A silver pickup behind me laid on the horn and I snapped alert. With a glance at the rear view mirror, I pulled ahead. I couldn't make out the driver so I just waved, assuming it was John, and pulled into the market parking lot. The silver truck ripped around me with a short squeak of tires and sped down the street.

Usually I had a list but I forgot to make one, so grocery shopping took a bigger bite out of the day. I thought about buying a bottle of wine, just in case, but since I normally don't drink wine, it might be a waste. Maybe that was counting my chickens a little too soon. I left it on the shelf. By the time I got checked out and the bags loaded up in a cart, almost an hour had passed.

I was mentally working through the jewelry that awaited my return and not paying any attention to my truck until I pushed the button to unlock the back hatch. I lifted the gate, grabbed a bag and started to load it in the back.

Then I saw my window.

The window on the passenger side was smashed - a gaping, wide open hole where the window had been.

I left the groceries and walked around the truck.

Chunks of safety glass covered the front seat and the floorboards. The glove compartment was hanging open. Papers littered the floor. I could see my registration laying on the seat, pulled out of the envelope and tossed on top of it.

Nothing else was damaged, that I could tell. I looked around the parking lot, hoping someone had seen what happened. Not a soul in sight. I stood there for several minutes, then pulled out my cell phone.

And you know which cop responded.

John was driving a squad car although not in uniform. When he got out of the car, his eyes were cool, calculating, almost like I was a stranger.

"Thought you were off today," I said.

"I was at the station when the call came in, heard the name, and volunteered to take the call."

"That was nice of you. I don't think there's anything you can do, but I wanted to report it, just in case. This is going to set me back some," I said, gesturing at the empty space where the window had been. "I didn't touch anything, in case you can get some prints."

"I doubt there will be fingerprints. Looks like a smash and grab," he said, walking around and looking in the other windows, all business now. "Anything missing? Did you have CD's out in sight?"

"No CD's, I don't keep them on the seat. The other stuff? I haven't really looked."

I went around to the back where I had been loading groceries. There was the last box of books and a couple of paper bags, all dumped over. The Lalique dishes, the Carnival glass pitcher, some other small glass items, were all scattered around, loose in the back, with wadded up balls of paper used for packing. Nothing looked damaged, more like someone was looking to see what had been in the bags and box.

"I can't really see where anything is missing," I said. "Someone has dumped my stuff out, unwrapped some of it. I think this is all there was. I had already taken most of it inside."

John leaned back into the cruiser and pulled a clipboard out of the car. He flipped a few pages and started writing on it.

"Can I get your driver's license number? I know your address," he said, one corner of his mouth lifting in a slight grin, the first sign of warmth he had shown since he arrived.

I pulled my license out and handed it over.

He was busy, writing things down, the sun glinting off his hair. I liked the way it fluttered in the breeze, the way his forehead creased as he worked, things I would not have noticed before last night.

He's lived across the drive for over a year and I was only now noticing how handsome he was. All the times he had come by to pay his rent, or I had waved across the street, I never really looked at him, kind of like looking at a map and not seeing the terrain.

He finished up and handed me back my license, along with his card, on which he had written a case number. My fingers brushed his as I took it and a spark jumped between us. Static electricity. I started, almost dropping the license but managing to hang on to it. I looked up at him to see if he noticed and there was that odd half grin.

"Not much else I can do," he said. "You can file with your insurance company. Give them this case number to prove you did file a police report. They can get anything else they need from us. We will provide a copy of the report if they request one. What's your deductible?"

"What?

He grinned, this time wide and friendly. "Deductible. The amount you have to pay before the insurance kicks in." His eyes twinkled now, bright and clear.

I could feel my cheeks get warm. "Oh, I think it's two hundred. Or maybe four. Not sure. I never filed a claim before."

"Check with your insurance company anyway, report it. You may have to pay for repairs yourself but at least you will have a record of payment, and should anything else happen to your truck this year, you have paid the deductible. Or at least part of it."

He reached out and ruffled my hair. "You should know this stuff. My duty as an officer to make you aware of it.

Have you got a camera on that fancy phone?" At my nod, he said, "Get a couple of pictures of the window and the inside of the truck for the insurance guys."

"Got it. And thank you."

"Just doing my duty, ma'am."

"Thank you anyway, John. I do appreciate it, you coming out." I stuck out my hand. No spark this time, thank heavens.

He shook my hand, held it a little longer than necessary. "Take care, Tee. I'll see you soon. I haven't forgotten I owe you a dinner."

With that, he got back in the squad car, backed up and drove out of the parking lot.

I could see why the single women wanted this guy. My little me bubble had excluded anyone else for so long I had become immune somewhere along the way.

Now I found myself wondering when, and if, we were going to have dinner again. His reputation preceded him. I wasn't sure if he meant it or was just exercising his natural talent for flirting.

I hoped he meant it.

I watched him out of sight, then turned back to my damaged truck. I left the groceries in the cart and pulled out my phone.

I took pictures of the broken window, the glass on the floorboards and front seat. I rolled the cart to the back of the truck, left it a little longer while I repacked the spilled boxes.

Nothing seemed to be broken so once they were packed, I loaded the groceries and headed for home.

After I put things away, I took a dustpan and a trash bag out to clean up the glass in my truck, glad it was safety glass. I didn't have to deal with shards and splinters. Once the glass was swept up and bagged, I brought the hand vacuum out and vacuumed the area to be on the safe side. When I finished I boxed up my other things and carried everything into the house.

I felt uneasy that someone had been in my truck, in my personal space. It left an uncomfortable feeling, like some kind of residue making my skin itch and crawl.

After the truck was cleaned up, I drove over to Mike's Motors, where I had bought the truck, to see about getting a new window. The guy there was nice, going out to look at my truck and commiserating with me on the damage.

He quoted me a price and suggested I leave the truck and they could get to it the next day. I signed the work order, handed over my keys, and started walking home, taking the long way around. Lunch was long past and I was hungry.

I swung over a block, avoiding the community park that took up half of the block, and walked down to Kelly's for a late lunch or early supper.

I ordered a bacon cheeseburger and a chocolate shake, figuring I'll walk that off getting home.

Flash.

Hey, Muse, how's it going?

Hey, Tim. Well so far my truck has been vandalized, the car dealer requires three hundred dollars to fix my truck, I don't know the deductible on my insurance and I am facing a long walk home.

What happened?

Someone broke the window out on my truck, dumped my stuff all over the back.

Anything taken? CD's, books, change?

I forgot to check the console. Could be change or CD's missing. Nothing that was on the seat, not that I saw anyway. Just made a mess and cost me money.

Probably kids.

Doesn't pay for the window. Why can't they mow lawns? Get a paper route?

That, my dear, doesn't begin to pay enough for two hundred dollar sneakers and a hundred dollar video game. Very expensive to be a kid these days.

So is my window.

Well, how was dinner?

Fine. Fun, really. Nice to have someone to talk to besides Dave and Cletus.

Present company accepted I assume. Oh, right, someone you can see.

You know what I mean, Tim.

So, are you going to do it again? Have him over for dinner?

Tentatively, yes. He said he'll cook next time.

That sounds positive. He must have enjoyed himself.

I hope so.

And the truck's in the shop? How long is it going to take to get the window fixed?

Probably tomorrow.

That's pretty good service. The walk will do you good. Get some exercise.

I get plenty of exercise, thank you. Lugging those boxes back and forth has given me arms like Arnie.

And the legs?

I do not have legs like a weight lifter.

Didn't think you did, just trying to get your mind off the truck.

Why me? Why would they break into my truck? You could see there was only a couple of paper bags and a box back there even with privacy glass.

Kids don't need a reason, Muse. Some just do it to see if they can get away with it, like some macho thing. Proves their manhood or something.

I catch them and I'll prove their manhood for them, give 'em a little boot right in the manhood.

Ouch, that's kind of harsh.

Not harsh enough.

The waitress was back with my burger, napkins and silverware. I ate a fry, added salt, and cut the burger in half.

You did file a report?

Yeah, I called the police, took pictures of the truck, filed a report and got a case number. The insurance lady said they would get me a check as soon as I sent them the receipt for the window repair, less my deductible.

Pretty good service I'd say.

She also assured me that my deductible was on record, in case any other accidents happen this year. With a reminder that the deductible will be due again next year. I've paid car insurance for twenty years this is my first claim, and she feels it's necessary to let me know I'll have to pay the deductible again next year.

Calm down, Muse. Standard procedure. She's just doing her job.

Yeah, yeah, still ticks me off. There were other cars in the lot and none of them were broken into. Only mine.

Consider it a compliment. Best looking vehicle in the lot. You may have been the only one with anything to play in. That's the advantage to a car, trunk space. Never know what's in the trunk.

My windows are tinted. It's not easy to see in the back.

Still, it could be seen. Might have been someone looking for something to pawn, or sell.

But nothing was taken. And that pitcher is worth some bucks.

How many people would know that? Especially kids. Consider yourself lucky they didn't just trash it completely.

I guess you're right.

You know I'm right. You take care of yourself, now, hear?

The frequency of Tim's visits added to the odd times he turned up was beginning to concern me.

Where before he was the nocturnal visitor, he now turned up any time of day, his questions and observations more pointed. He was taking on a distinct personality, with views not necessarily my own. Maybe it was time to think about that psychologist.

Lord knows I had every other kind of doctor in my address book and on my phone.

I finished my lunch while talking to Tim, so I picked up my check, left a tip, and went to the counter to pay.

Walking home I thought about what Tim said.

In some ways I was lucky. I still had my stuff, and the window could be fixed. I also decided not to leave things in my truck any more. From now on as soon as I got home everything went inside, either in the house or the garage.

The rest of the way home I thought about John. I really enjoyed his company the other night and looked forward to seeing him again, hopefully when I wasn't stammering and blushing like a school girl.

Being human, I also wondered how the single ladies of Monarch Beach were going to take the news that I had dinner with the town's hot guy. And there was a good chance I was going to do it again.

I smiled all the way home.

Chapter Five

With no truck I spent the next morning cataloging all the items from the weekend, sorting through the books I wanted to keep, and boxing up the stuff that I couldn't use.

The glassware for Andy was wrapped up again and boxed, to drop off after my truck was fixed. Everything was cataloged and on the computer. I changed the memory card in my camera, to preserve the pictures of the smashed window.

Once that was all done, I backed the files up online, to a secure site that kept my records.

By the time I cleaned up my desk Mike's called that the truck was ready.

The morning marine layer had burned off and the weather was warming up, at least till the breeze picked up off the ocean. Nice day for a walk.

I grabbed my camera and stuck it in my fanny pack. I might get some good pictures on a day like this. Buckling on the pack, I locked the front door and headed uptown to retrieve my wheels.

Half way to Mike's I noticed a silver pickup idling along behind me, maybe looking for a parking place. I turned to look, hoping it was John and I could get a lift the rest of the way.

No such luck. The truck turned at the intersection.

About four blocks from the repair shop was a small park, with a fenced area for dogs. I cut through there, stopped to admire the dogs playing, leaning against the fence for a brief rest.

Maybe I was out of shape. Never going to admit it. With Tim, I couldn't even think it, in case he was there and I wasn't aware of him.

I left the dogs behind, continuing my walk.

Then I stopped. I realized I had gone the wrong way.

This end of the park was new to me, much more wooded and overgrown. I could still hear street noise close by.

Weaving through the tree trunks I made my way deeper into the wooded area until a hedge about waist high blocked my path.

Grumbling under my breath I looked around for an alternative route. It was either go back the way I had come and go around the block, or go through the bushes. Wearing a sweatshirt and jeans I was fairly sure I could get through without permanent damage. Looking for the easiest way, I held my arms up out of the way and waded into the bushes.

WHOMP!

Something heavy hit me in the back and I hit the ground. With my arms up over my head I had no way to break my fall.

I fell flat on my face, my head on the other side of the hedge, getting a mouth full of pine needles and dead leaves, all the gray bits and pieces that rest under bushes.

Spitting and spraying I flung my head around, trying to clear my mouth while wondering what had hit me.

A heavy weight was still pressing me into the ground, pulling and pushing my body, like elbows and knees grinding me into the dirt.

Panic set in, the will to survive.

I fought back, kicking, twisting, and struggling. Adrenaline poured into my system. I began to buck and heave, snarking up dirt and leaves, coughing, scrabbling with my hands and knees, clawing at the ground with my fingers, trying to dislodge this thing on my back. Bushes and branches struck and stung while I fought, twisting sideways, pushing with my knees, clawing with my hands, elbows digging.

I was fighting so hard to breathe, I was unable to scream.

Suddenly the weight was gone.

With the weight off my back, my hands and knees caught and I scurried out of the bushes, crab like, still kicking, spitting out dirt.

I broke out the other side, my momentum carrying me three or four feet clear of the bushes, onto the grass.

I lay gasping and wheezing, still trying to clear my mouth, my eyes wide trying to see everywhere at once, not knowing what the hell happened.

I spit and swiped my mouth, feeling my lip starting to swell where I had banged it on the ground during my fall. Even my teeth hurt.

Scooting backward, I managed to open a bigger space between me and the bushes.

The sudden jar when I hit the ground had given me a headache, my whole body burned with scratches and welts although I didn't think anything was broken.

Looking around, I saw no one, or anything that could have slammed into me. I levered myself up and got to my feet, brushed off my legs and the front of my sweatshirt, swatting at my hair, imagining spiders crawling around building nests. Ugh.

I could hear faint traffic sounds and the dogs at play back where I had rested. Bending over, I put my hands on my knees, and tried to calm my racing heart, counting off my breaths.

The sleeve of my sweat shirt was ripped, the skin on my arm scratched and bleeding but not severely. Muscles I didn't know I had were complaining. Both my hands were scratched and scraped, three nails broken, one of which was showing blood where it ripped off. There was a small tear in the knee of my jeans.

I hurt all over.

Pulling up my sweat shirt I could see where branches had scratched my skin. Although nothing looked serious, they were all red and angry, a patchwork of marks all over my chest and belly. My jeans had protected my legs somewhat, except for my knee.

Looking around I still saw nothing - not a person, a dog, anything that could have slammed into my back. I straightened up slowly and looked over the bushes, to the other side.

Perhaps a huge branch had fallen? Maybe something big fell out of the trees?

There was nothing. The grass was scuffed up in clumps, a few divots on the surface. No branch.

The adrenaline rush was gone, leaving me weaker than I had been since chemo. My knees were shaking, threatening to give way. I gave a final swipe at my hair and shook out my shirt, brushing off my sleeves.

I stumbled a little getting my legs to get me the hell out of there. I could feel a place on my back, stinging more than the others, right at my waistline.

Right where the fanny pack should be.

It wasn't there.

I spun in a wobbly circle looking all around me, forgetting the pain in my back.

Stepping back to the hedge, using my feet and knees to shove aside the brush, I looked around the ground.

No pack.

What the heck? It had to be here somewhere. Only it wasn't. Not on the ground, not stuck in a bush. Nowhere.

I pulled my phone out of my pocket. It seemed to be okay, the screen wasn't broken or anything. It lit up as soon as I opened it. Good thing I made a practice of keeping it in my pocket and not in the pack.

Feeling the scratch on my back made me realize the cut went right through my sweatshirt. My fingers could poke through a tear over the burning place in my back.

When I brought my hand back to my face there were blood smears across my fingers.

No way was I going back through that brush.

Too shaken to jog, I headed the same direction I had been going and aimed for the sidewalk as fast as I could limp along, checking over my shoulder constantly to make sure no one was behind me, or lurking behind a tree.

Reaching the street, I paused to catch my breath, fighting the nausea that threatened to throw my lunch all over the sidewalk.

There were people here - two women chatting a few yards up the street, a guy leaning on his car and talking on his cell.

None of them paid the least attention to me.

I called the police.

Again.

I wasn't sure the officer who responded was old enough to drive. He pulled the standard little notebook out of his shirt pocket, listened to my story, and made a few notes. At the point in my story where I said my back was hurt, he reached out and turned me away from him, gently lifting my shirt.

"You have a pretty good scratch here," he said. "Could your pack be on a branch over there? Show me where you fell."

We made our way back across the street and into the woody edge of the park.

It was easy to see where I had come through the bushes.

Twigs and leaves all over the grass, broken branches - it looked like a large animal had crashed through. He kicked around in the bushes a while, even shoving his way through to the other side and looking around over there.

I was beginning to lose patience.

"I told you, I looked. It's not here."

"Yes, ma'am".

He shoved his way back through the hedge. At this rate, there was going to be a permanent path for the next guy to happen along.

"I can file a report. There's not much else I can do right now." He proffered his card. "This is my card. This number here is the report number, if you need to reference it in the future. If you have any more problems, you can call that number."

He pocketed the notebook and pen. "I can request extra patrols in the area, ma'am, but I think this is just an isolated incident. You're sure you had the fanny pack?"

With an eye roll he could probably hear, I said yes, I was sure.

"Do you want an ambulance? Have that scratch looked at?"

"No, thanks," I sighed. "Thank you for coming out."

"Can I give you a ride to your vehicle?"

"You know what, yes, you can. I'm through walking for the day."

~~~

After I got my truck and paid for the new window, I went straight home.

I pulled off my shirt and jeans and twisted around to see my back in the bathroom mirror while the shower warmed up. A dozen scratches covered my back.

The largest one, the one that really hurt, was four or five inches long, a straight line. The skin was broken, raw and angry looking, but not deep.

I got in the shower and sucked in my breath when the hot water hit it.

It was a short shower. When I got out I dabbed ointment on the scratches I could reach, managing to smear a gob on my back to cover the large one. Then it was sweatshirt, clean jeans and thick socks.

Grabbing up the soiled clothes, I carried them downstairs to the washer, tossed them inside and started the cycle.

In the kitchen I put on the kettle, got down a teapot, added tea and waited for the water to boil. While waiting I swallowed a couple of Tylenol.

My camera was a lost cause since I had no insurance on it. Luckily I had another one, an older model. Digital cameras are not that expensive any more, very decent ones can be bought fairly cheap.

The question was why would someone want the one I had? It was certainly not worth a lot. For that matter how would anyone know my camera was in the fanny pack? Maybe mistake the shape for a phone or tablet of some kind? A huge wad of cash I rolled up and stashed on my fanny?

And why this rush of things happening to me? The truck, now this. I gave up. I didn't know what was going on, and right now, didn't care.

Taking my tea into the living room, I pulled down the afghan, covered up and turned on the TV. Mindless entertainment is my comfort food.

I drank my tea while watching an old Clark Gable movie, then pulled up the afghan and snuggled in to nurse my aches and pains. Somewhere along the line I drifted into a nap.

FLASH

Hey, Muse. What's going on?

Definitely not my day.

Were you asleep? You sound sleepy.

Napping.

This time of day? You all right?

Yes I'm all right. Just another one of those stupid things that keep happening to me, and I am really getting tired of it.

Now, what happened?

I got mugged on the way to get my truck. My pack got stolen, with my camera inside.

Are you okay? Are you hurt?

Just scratches. More pissed off than anything. And don't try to tell me it was kids, not this time. It was someone big, and heavy.

You have stepped in something, girl, and it's followed you home.

And what does that mean?

Once may be random. Twice in two days begins to look deliberate.

I figured that much out myself.

Oh, testy. Okay, back up. Start from the beginning.

I got up this morning and went to get my truck. There's a park along the way and I cut through there. I had to push through a hedge to get to the next street and something or someone hit me in the back and knocked me down. When I got back on my feet I had a fat lip, a big scratch on my back, lots of little scratches, things in my hair and a bad attitude.

But you're all right? Did you call the cops? Report it?

Yes I did for what little good it will do. I didn't see anything.

Was it your cop you called?

I don't have a cop, Tim. No, it was another guy, one that didn't look old enough to shave.

Hey, just asking. Kind of funny that the new guy comes over for dinner and then your truck gets vandalized and you get mugged. You've lived across from him for over a year and barely spoke, now you can't turn around without stepping on the guy's toe. Lot of coincidence there. I don't much care for coincidence.

I thought for a few minutes.

John has nothing to do with it. Why would he? What possible reason could he have for trashing my truck? Because I asked him to help me move a piece of furniture? Be serious.

Just pointing out that this all happened after he came for dinner. You sure he's a cop?

Yes, he's a cop. I've seen him in a squad car, I've taken him to the station, seen him at breakfast with other cops. He's a cop. I even have one of his business cards. He gave it to me when he filed the report on my truck.

Whoa, defensive there, Muse. Cool down. Think for a minute.

About what? That somebody messed up my truck, and now stole my camera. Got it. I was there. I have the cuts and bruises to show it.

You're sure you're okay? Did you bump your head?

Didn't even skin my knees although they are sore as hell. It was in the dirt. Just scratches from the bushes, and the big one on my back,

Could it be a cut? On your back?

I took a look in the mirror, looks like a bigger scratch. Longer, not deeper.

Sounds like someone may have cut the belt on your pack, to get the camera.

Even if they did, there was nothing in the pack. The camera was maybe thirty bucks new. Nothing else worth anything. My camera, some tissues, Chapstick, pen and paper, just little crap no one would want.

You have something someone wants. What all did you buy last weekend?

Two, no, three boxes of books, the hall tree, a box of cheap jewelry, all from Mildred's. I bought a glass pitcher at another sale and a couple of small decorative dishes earlier, and that's it.

All that is still here? In your house?

No, not all of it. I sold the hall tree to Andy and he picked that up the same day. I have the books here. I listed the ones that had some value, put them on the shelves and boxed up the ones that I couldn't sell. The books are still here but why would someone want the books?

Books wouldn't fit in a fanny pack.

A paperback would, but they're old, and they all listed. Most expensive was twenty bucks.

Well, sweetheart, you have something someone wants. That's my take on it. Whoever broke into the truck could have gotten your address from your registration. You make sure you lock up tight.

There was a knock at the door. I stood up too fast and had to grab the arm of the couch for a minute.

"Coming," I called.

Gotta go.

Company?

Someone at the door.

Shiny new quarter says it's the cop.

Stop it, Tim.

We'll see. I'm out.

I got to the front door and opened it.

John smiled back at me.

"Are you all right?"

"I'm okay," I said, gesturing him inside. "Just scratched up, some bumps and bruises."

"I read the report." He took a seat on the couch. He was wearing jeans and a sweat shirt again. "Fill me in. Where were you?"

Shoving Dave off the couch, I folded up the afghan and sat down, already feeling the bruises and aches, arms and legs stiffening up, sorer now than when I first laid down.

"I was walking back uptown to get my truck. I cut through that wooded place, the end of the park, instead of walking around. Someone or something pushed me down through the bushes. Whoever it was took the fanny pack, with my camera inside, and took off. I never even heard them coming. Or leaving. It was just wham, bam, thank you ma'am and gone."

"Did you see anyone? Was anyone behind you earlier?"

I sighed. "I have been over it and over it, John. If there was someone there, I didn't notice. I mean, there were people on the sidewalk, people walking dogs, watering lawns, just all the usual. I didn't see anyone I knew. I would have noticed that. I cut through the park to save some time, it's not my usual walk."

"You're sure you didn't just lose the pack? Before you ever got to the park?"

I thought for a minute before answering.

"I'm not positive about anything," I admitted. "It was buckled on when I left the house. I think I would have noticed, or felt it, if it fallen off. It would have made a noise if it hit the sidewalk, with the camera inside. No, I don't think it fell off anywhere."

He sat back, a slight frown on his face. "It's just an odd coincidence. The truck Monday, now this. Have you made anyone angry recently?"

"Not that I know of," I said. "I mean, I don't really have that much interaction with people. I talk to Andy, on the phone. I see Sharon a couple of times a week, the folks at Kelly's. I don't see that many people in any given week."

I realized how pathetic that sounded. I really had no social life. The occasional beer with Sharon and some friends at the Gem, stopping by Andy's store, that was about it. Most of my business was done online.

"Any strange phone calls?"

"No, none I remember. I have a land line here for business, and it's connected to the answering machine. Friends and family call my cell. I mostly use the house phone for the internet connection."

"What about customers? Do any of them come here? To the house?"

"No. That's a definite rule. I don't give out my address, to anyone, ever. If I have to meet anyone, for any reason, I would have them meet me at Andy's store."

"How about your truck? Do you garage it at night?"

"Very rarely. I have shelves in the garage for my inventory. There's room for the truck, but I seldom park in there. I don't usually have anything in the truck. Besides, I live across the drive from a cop. How much safer could it be?"

He smiled at that. "Okay," he stood up. "I'll keep an eye out. Hopefully, this is the end of it."

I followed him to the door and opened it.

He stepped out to the porch, then turned back toward me.

"Be careful, Tee. And you're right. You do live right across from a cop. If you need me, just holler. I sleep light."

He was giving me that look again, measuring, calculating. "I'm serious. If you need me, call."

"Noted, sir. I just hope this is all random and I'm being a nervous Nellie."

"I don't think you're the nervous type, Tee. You strike me as very self-sufficient. Just be extra cautious."

"Will do. Have a good evening, John. Thanks for stopping by."

He gave me a salute, turned, and made his way across the lawn to his own house.

Good to know you're there, I thought, shutting the door. I flipped the lock, and then the dead bolt. Then I went back and checked to be sure the back door was locked, making a mental note to be more careful locking up.

Waking up the next morning my body reminded me of my misadventure. Muscles ached, bruised knees hurt, scratches on my arms, chest and back all stung.

Rolling over to sit up on the side of the bed, my back was stiff and sore. Great way to start the day.

The mirror confirmed the way I felt. My lip was swollen, one eye sported a shiner and there was a noticeable bruise along my jaw.

Someone was sure to ask how the other guy looked. All I could hope was that somewhere in the squabble I had connected with enough force to have left my own marks on that other guy.

Cletus and Dave were concerned they would miss breakfast, as evidenced by them rubbing all over me, butting with their heads to get me moving.

"Give me a minute, guys" I pleaded. They weren't going for it. I got to my feet, slid into my slippers, and pulled on the oversize sweat shirt that serves as a bath robe.

Shuffling along, I made it to the kitchen and fed the cats, got the coffee pot going, then shuffled back upstairs for a hot shower.

The shower helped ease sore muscles, ointment helped the scratches. Dressed and shod, the smell of fresh coffee drew me back to the kitchen.

There's something about that first cup of coffee in the morning. Everything looks better. Too sore to sit, I stood over the sink and sipped the hot brew, looking out the window.

The lawn was wet with dew, still silver in the shade and undisturbed, a sure sign that autumn was near.

Across the drive John's truck glistened, wet with the morning dew.

For over a year he had been right there across the drive, waving or nodding when we saw each other, politely dropping off his rental check every month. I had talked to him more in the past two weeks than I had in a year.

I refilled my cup and stiffly made my way back to the couch in the living room. Picking up my Kindle I carefully settled in for a lazy day. The cats joined me as soon as I spread the afghan over my legs. I reached for the remote.

It was early evening by the time I finally roused myself from a day spent dozing on the couch, wrapped in the afghan, reading and watching old movies. Lunch had been cheese and crackers, a couple of cookies and an apple, nothing requiring me to move around much or stand for long.

Nice way to spend a day but now I was hungry.

Cleaning up the empty cups and paper plates decorating the coffee table and carrying them to the kitchen took two trips. By that time I was moving better, not nearly as stiff or sore as this morning.

I was standing with the refrigerator open trying to decide on something for supper when there was a knock at the front door.

I opened the door to find John standing there, balancing a big pizza box on a six pack of beer. The smells from the pizza were enough to make me bite him.

Instead I stepped aside and motioned him in.

"I thought you might not want to cook," he said, following me to the kitchen where I got down paper plates and napkins.

"You were exactly right," I said, handing him a plate holder. "You are my favorite person as of right now. To be fair, that may change when the pizza is gone."

When he reached to take the proffered items I held out I noticed the back of his hand was scraped and angry looking, the knuckles looking swollen.

"Whoa, what happened to your hand?" I asked. "You look as bad as me."

He glanced down at his hand, turning it so it was palm up. "Chasing a guy last night," he smiled. "He looks worse than I do." He took two pieces of pizza and put them on his plate. "I hope you like everything on your pizza. I figured you could just take off anything you don't like."

I sat two beers on the counter and put the other four in the refrigerator.

"Everything is fine, as long as that means no anchovies," I said, opening one beer and taking a long drink. It was still cold and crisp. I slid a piece of the pie onto my plate and sat down at the counter across from him.

"We have that in common," he said, chewing on a slice, "not a fan of the little fishes."

With my mouth full of spicy pepperoni and hot melted cheese it was hard to talk so I just nodded.

The pizza was delicious. We chewed away for a few minutes dabbing away with napkins and making those little happy sounds you make when the food is good.

Pausing to swallow some beer I noticed his hand again, this time the other one. It, too, was scratched and scraped.

Seeing that I was looking at his hands he set down the slice he was holding and reached for his beer.

"One of the hazards of the job," he said, flexing his fingers. "It looks worse than it is."

"Oh, I believe that," I said, displaying my own scratched hands and forearms. "I spent the whole day on the couch. I was just figuring out what to eat when you showed up." I grinned at him. "My hero."

He chuckled and picked up his pizza, relaxing back in his chair as he ate. "You can't go wrong with a good pizza. Besides, I think it was my turn to provide dinner." He looked at me, his eyes unreadable. "Now I'm off the hook and its back to your turn."

I thought about that for a second and dropped my eyes so he couldn't see how much I liked that idea.

"Any news on the park?" I wiped my hands on a napkin and reached for the beer.

"Nope. I even checked back, talked to a couple of the guys, old timers on the force. The last problem we had there was 4th of July. That was a couple of fist fights, drunk and disorderly, the usual holiday stuff, and even that was at the other end of the park, down by the picnic tables."

"I can use my old camera, so no big loss," I said. "It just ticks me off."

"Believe me," he said, seriously, "it could have been a lot worse."

We finished the pizza with small talk, weather, that sort of thing, eating all but two slices. At last, I dropped a crust on my plate and wiped my hands, heaving a huge satisfied sigh.

"That was perfect. Thank you so much."

"My pleasure," he said, wiping his own hands and draining his beer. "I was going to get pizza anyway. I'm glad you liked it."

Together we picked up and cleaned up the counter. I wrapped the remaining slices in foil for him to take home.

"This was nice," he said when he was standing by the door. "We should get together more often. I get tired of eating alone. It usually comes down to something between two pieces of bread or Kelly's. Too much trouble to cook for one person."

"I know what you mean," I agreed, holding the door for him. "You sure you don't want those last two beers?"

"No, thanks. You keep them. I can always borrow one if I want one." He grinned at me again and I couldn't meet that direct gaze.

"That you can do, any time," I smiled, looking at his shirt. "And I keep a pretty good pantry, so if you're hungry, come on over. I can always throw something together even if it's only bacon and eggs."

He gave me one of those long looks, like he was measuring me for something. "I may take you up on that, too," he said, and I knew I was blushing, felt it from my neck up.

We said our goodbyes and I closed the door behind him, watching through the window as he made his way across the lawn.

Strange that we both got hurt at the same time. I never really thought about the police getting bruised up, although common sense would tell you that they aren't super men. Of course they get bruised, and scraped, and shot at.

On occasion they even get hit.

I was sure glad he showed up with supper. And I was pretty sure he was flirting tonight, not just being neighborly. Turning off the lights, I made my way upstairs to get ready for bed. John was still on my mind as I drifted to sleep so I guess it's a good thing Tim didn't show up.

~~~

The next morning I was moving a little better, not nearly as sore although not ready to run a marathon in the near future. I retrieved the morning paper while the coffee brewed. Our local paper only comes out on Thursday.

I sat at the kitchen table sipping my coffee while I read the ads, marking any that looked interesting.

The Baptist church was having a rummage sale on Friday, the Friends of the Library were having a book sale, both worth a look. Although I didn't feel like making it a full day I knew I had to get out there for a little while tomorrow.

Today I could afford to take it easy, spend another day around the house, with hot tea and Tylenol.

The next morning I was up, showered and ready to go. I gathered my gear and headed out.

The first four sales weren't worth stopping at, being mostly clothes and baby stuff, none of which interested me.

The next one I stopped at yielded two boxes of old paperbacks, including another box of Dell map back paperbacks which are collectible and getting harder and harder to find. On the plus side, these were also very clean and nice.

So many old books smell of mildew or old cigarette smoke. Smell is almost impossible to get out of paper.

When I had the boxes loaded up I decided that would keep me busy for a while and headed to Kelly's to meet Sharon.

The library book sale could wait till after lunch. I was interested in old books and they weren't as popular as the new stuff. They would still be there.

I was lucky enough to find a parking space right in front.

Sharon had her usual booth towards the back, fourth from the door, her coffee and the newspaper folded in front of her. She waved at me and I made my way back, grabbing a cup from the tray by the door.

When I was settled and Sally had filled my cup, Sharon leaned back and gave me a grin.

"So what did you do for dinner last night?" She looked like the cat with the bird in its belly, her green eyes bright.

"I had pizza," I answered, stirring cream into my coffee.

"Uh-huh," she smiled. "And what else?"

I tried to look blank, then broke into a grin. "Okay, John brought pizza over last night. How'd you know?"

She chuckled. "I was there when he came to pick it up."

"I didn't know you knew him," I said.

"Honey, it's a small town. Every single gal in town knows John Kincaid. Half of them monitor his movements, although I'm not one of them. Besides I've seen him when I was at your place. Waved or said hey."

"Oh, okay. Have you dated him?"

"Nope, I never had the chance. I would have jumped had that carrot been dangled."

"Pretty fickle, huh? Him, not you," I added quickly.

Sharon leaned forward and dropped her voice. "Honey, he's a love 'em and leave 'em kind of guy. He's dated a lot of gals in town. As soon as they think they have something going, he's out the door and down the road."

"Last year," she continued, looking around to see if anyone was close, "there was an incident." She lifted a brow. "One that was shut up pretty quick by the department."

100

I couldn't help myself. "What happened?"

"Some girl tried to kill herself, right on the steps of the station. Cut her wrists. Fortunately, another cop noticed and called 911, got her some help. The cuts weren't that deep but it still made the news."

"What's that got to do with John?"

"She was one he dumped. She had a letter pinned to her shirt, with his name on the front. All very dramatic. Made the evening news." She leaned back. "No one ever found out what it said, but he was given a warning by the City Council. I think that's probably why he quit dating around here."

"That wasn't his fault she decided to pull something like that."

"Agreed. She had to have problems before he came along. I think she even had a record of suicide attempts or something like that. Still, didn't do his reputation any good. That's why you were news, sweetie. John hasn't been more than polite to anyone local in quite a while."

I thought for a minute, then saw Sally coming and changed the subject.

"It was just a pizza, and he's a neighbor. Besides all that, he was hungry."

"He eats here a lot, too," said Sally, joining us. "So how was dinner?"

"You too? Does everyone know?"

"It's Friday, sweetie. Sharon has been here almost an hour already." She grinned. "So how was it?"

I sighed. "Very nice. He brought a pizza and beer, we ate, we talked and he left. That's it."

"Second time," said Sally. "Good going, you're doing better than the rest of them. What can I get you? The special is fish and chips." She held her pencil at the ready. "We don't have a good looking cop to serve it, you're gonna have to make do with me."

I stuck my tongue out at her. "Bacon cheeseburger for me, no fries."

"I'll have the hot meat loaf sandwich," said Sharon, "And iced tea. I think I've had enough coffee."

Sally left to place our orders.

"Now," said Sharon, settling back, "how did it go?"

"It was fine, Sharon, seriously. It was very thoughtful of him. I enjoy his company. That was it."

"What did you talk about?"

"Books, movies, pizza," I said. "Why all the interest?"

"Because. You haven't had a private life in years, other than meeting up with us at the Gem once in a while. You haven't been to a movie, a Tupperware party, anything. This is news."

"Do they still have Tupperware parties?" I asked with a grin.

Now it was Sharon who stuck out her tongue. Are we adult or what?

"Imagine my surprise when I remark on a large pizza and a six pack for one guy, and the guy says it's for my best friend, who, by the way, did not mention that she was attacked yesterday in a public park, or that she was having dinner with a good looking neighbor."

"I didn't know," I said. "Complete surprise. I opened the door and there he was, pizza and beer in hand. And I really appreciated it since I was not feeling my best. It was very thoughtful of him."

She leaned forward to pat my hand. "Very thoughtful," she said. "He seems to be a really nice guy and you sure as hell deserve it after this last two years. I'm just teasing you. Now," she sat back again "what happened in the park?"

By the time I brought her up to date Sally had brought our lunches.

"There's apple or peach pie for dessert. I asked if there was a good looking cop on the back burner but you're going to have to settle for the pie."

As I reached for the ketchup I hoped I hadn't put John back in a spotlight he so obviously wanted to avoid.

There are several drawbacks to living alone. One, is that you have no one to talk to except yourself, which is kind of frowned on by the general public. A pet will ease that unless it's a goldfish, which will cause the same reaction with the general public.

I felt lucky to have Tim, even if I did not introduce him around.

The second one is cooking. There are not a lot of recipes for one serving. I thought about checking Amazon for a one person cookbook. Maybe I should consider writing one.

The alternative is a large pot of something divided up over several days. That, too, will pale about the fourth day of soup, stew, or chili.

My solution so far has been sandwiches, and take out. Pizza and Chinese pretty much cover the takeout and again, you have the leftovers.

The final option is eating out, which can be expensive if not moderated. This explains why I often have a big lunch at Kelly's and a take away box for leftovers, which gets labeled supper.

Also why I bought supper when John came over.

It now appeared to be my turn again. Pizza was out. I was going to have to cook. If, indeed, we were going to have supper together again. Maybe I better start looking for cookbooks.

I went by the Friends of the Library sale and snagged a couple of bags of books. They rarely have old books, hardback or paperback, which are my bread and butter. They did however have a table of cookbooks in varying sizes. I selected a couple of smaller ones from the fifties, hoping to be inspired by the time I was called on to cook. Perhaps there might also be a couple of one serving dishes.

During chemo your taste buds go whacko along with a lot of other things. Sometimes the effects go away immediately after the last treatment. Sometimes they don't go away, you get to keep them as a souvenir.

Another fatality is appetite, which takes a long time to come back. If you care, the cooking channels on TV will help cure that one. Just keeping it on in the background stimulates your appetite and will bring it back much faster.

A nurse told me about that one, and I am the first to admit, it made a difference with me.

All these thoughts about food made my own appetite kick start so I decided to call it a day.

I didn't want to cook and I was out anyway, so I drove over the ridge to Jade Beach, right next door to Monarch, and bought some Chinese food. I loaded up the brown paper bag and headed back home.

I slowed at the big curve on top of the ridge and behind me a pickup had to hit the brakes, hard enough to squeak. I waved him ahead, trying to see if it was John driving but the afternoon glare blinded my view inside.

I hoped it wasn't John headed home. I only ordered enough for one.

I had lugged the books into my office, showered, dressed in sweats and fed the cats. With the chores done I set out the cartons of Chinese and pulled down a plate.

I barely started filling it when my phone rang, the one in the living room, which is usually business. My friends call my cell.

I answered the phone.

No one there.

I know this happens to all of us but it's particularly irritating when you're in the middle of something else, such as pre-nuptial arrangements with your dinner.

Half way back to the kitchen the phone rang again.

Spinning back into the living room I snatched up the receiver and in a less than professional voice said hello.

Nothing.

After several hellos and no response, I put the phone back and went to get my dinner. There was a machine on that phone, let it answer.

I had important things to do.

Eat.

The phone rang again that night when I was already tucked in with the cats and the Kindle so I made no effort to get up and get it.

Another hang-up.

Great. I didn't owe anyone any money and my next doctor's appointment was a month away. If it was that important someone would leave a message.

FLASH

Hey, Muse, how are you?

Hey Tim, Where've you been?

Around the world and back again. Are you feeling better?

Yeah, I'm fine. Just stiff and sore.

Nothing else happened?

Nope. Other than some hang ups on my landline things have been back to normal. Hit some sales, lunch with Sharon, just the usual.

What hang ups?

Someone calling the house phone. No one there when I answer it. Probably kids or something.

How's the cop?

He's good I guess. He brought over a pizza the other night, had dinner.

Ah, a new man in the picture.

No, nothing like that. Just a neighbor doing something nice. He's banged up too, chasing some guy in the line of duty.

Banged up? As in how? Scratched up? Skinned knees?

I didn't see his knees, Tim. His hands were scratched up from rolling around on the asphalt with a bad guy.

I love you, Muse, but you are really thick headed some times.

What?

All these things that happened to you have been since you asked this guy to help move furniture. Your truck gets trashed, you get attacked in the park, and Mr. Wonderful suddenly wants to eat dinner with you every night. Too many coincidences. I don't believe it.

That's not fair, Tim, totally unnecessary.

Can't run out and slam the door can ya?

No, but I can go to sleep.

Listen to me, babe. Be careful around this guy, okay? He's been across the drive for a year and never bothered to bring pizza. Can't hurt to slow down some, right? I just want you to be safe. What do you really know about him?

I know he was an MP in the military and a deputy sheriff somewhere around LA. His dad lives over in the valley, his sister has come to visit a couple of times from LA. He's divorced, no kids, and has no pets. Now what else do you want to know?

I was getting really cranky, which is silly when you're talking to yourself.

Mad?

Tired. I need to get some rest.

Ok, ok, I get the hint. Just be careful. You've had enough on your plate.

I will, Tim. Believe me, I don't want to go through that again. And I sure as heck can't afford to keep repairing the truck.

Did you garage it tonight?

No, but I will start.

Good idea, even if it is mine. Get some rest, we'll talk again soon.

Night, Tim.

Night, Muse. Sleep well.

Chapter Six

By the following Friday I was feeling pretty good. The biggest scratch on my back was healing, the smaller ones scabbed over and the bruises reaching a nice lavender shade.

The books were sorted and listed, the spread sheet filled out and forwarded to my online base.

I still do the books for two small businesses and I got them up to date, sent their reports.

Caught up, I made a second pot of coffee, sat down with the ads and took a break.

Nothing interesting in the ads.

I had only seen John once all week, and that was to wave at as he left when I was pulling into my drive. I admit I was disappointed. I hoped he would show up for dinner again, or at least come by and borrow a book. He had several reasons to stop by if he needed one.

With a sigh, I realized I was reading a lot into a pizza.

I also found myself checking every silver pickup I saw, and let me tell you, they seemed to be everywhere. I always saw at least one every time I left the house.

Sharon called in the afternoon. She wanted to meet up at the Gem about seven and since I hadn't been out for a while, I decided to join her. We always wound up with a group, one more advantage to living in a small town most of your life. There was always someone you knew to dance with or share a beer.

The bar was originally called The Gem of the Coast, but over the years the locals shortened it to the Gem, mostly because people liked to say they were going to the Gem, knowing it sounded like they were going to the gym. To hear us talk, tourists must think we are the most workout conscious people on the coast.

The cats were fed and settled in on the afghan, the doors and windows locked and double checked. Grabbing my keys I headed out to the truck.

I don't as a rule carry a purse. I have a metal business card case that fits snugly in the back pocket of my jeans and contains my debit card, the rarely used credit card, driver's license and proof of insurance and my medical cards. Beats having to worry about a purse.

I left a lamp on in the living room, the front porch light on, and double checked the lock on the front door. Good to go. I was just getting into my truck when headlights turned into our main drive.

I looked up as John stopped across my driveway

"Headed out?" he asked through the lowered truck window.

"Meeting friends at the Gem," I said, and then for no earthly reason added, "Would you like to join us? It's really casual." I could feel a blush climbing up my neck and was glad it was dark.

I'm from the generation that waits for the guy to make an invitation.

John looked at me. The silence stretched. Finally he sighed. "I might do that. How long you going to be there?"

"No set time really. We usually stay till eleven or so."

He seemed to be considering. "I've got a few things to take care of," he said. "If it's not too late, I'll swing by."

"Great," I said, feeling like an idiot, 'hope to see you later."

"Be careful," he said, rolling up the window and turning into his driveway.

I started my truck and backed out, giving him a wave as I pulled out toward the street. I couldn't believe I did that. I really hoped I didn't make him uncomfortable with the invitation. Oh, well, too late now.

I pointed the truck toward downtown.

~~~

My usual bunch had the big corner table at the Gem. Made them easy to find, although Sharon's laugh could be heard for half a block.

I took the empty chair next to her and greeted the gang. It had been a while since I had seen everyone so I was deluged with questions about the incident in the park.

"Get some pepper spray," suggested Cora. "You can get one of those small ones and carry it on your key chain or a belt loop."

"Get a dog," said Greg.

Other suggestions were thrown out, drinks were ordered and talk resumed around the table. The juke box was blasting out old Garth Brooks hits, some couples were dancing while others were just chatting.

A typical Friday night at the Gem.

It's a local hangout, often featuring live music from local garage bands, cold beer, pizza and sandwiches, nothing fancy. Everyone danced with everyone else, ate off each other's plates and zinged in one liners at every opportunity, kind of a community social.

Sharon had asked first thing if I had seen John, and again, I explained that he lived across the drive so I had to see him. I busied myself drinking beer.

"That's not what I meant, and you know it," she said. "Have you seen him socially? Have you talked to him?"

"Not really, mostly hey how's it going, that kind of thing." I took a breath and blurted, "I did invite him to swing by tonight."

Sharon almost choked on her beer. "You did? Good for you! Do you think he will?"

"Probably not, it was a spur of the minute thing," I peeled a corner of the label on the beer bottle. "He's pretty gun shy about invitations."

She patted my shoulder. "Honey, every gal in town knows that."

I thought about that, knowing she was right. I could feel my spirits sink a little, surprised at how much I hoped he might show up.

It was half an hour later when Sharon leaned over and said, "Look who's here."

I glanced toward the entrance and there was John, to the side, his back to us, talking to one of the bouncers.

While I was watching him he turned and caught me looking at him. I was so happy to see him I didn't try to hide it, just gave him a huge smile.

He was wearing jeans and a plaid shirt with his shirt sleeves rolled up, and cowboy boots. He smiled back at me, a real honest to goodness smile that melted me where I sat.

Still holding my gaze he made his way through the dancing couples, straight to our table.

"Hey," I said when he joined us, knowing everyone was staring and not caring. "Pull up a chair."

He snagged a chair from another table. Sharon and I both slid over to make room for him between us.

"I think you know Sharon," I said. At his nod, I introduced him around the table to the others. Greg was making a beer run and John added his request to the order. He reached for his wallet and Greg waved it away.

"I'm glad you could make it," I said, knowing he could see that for himself.

He had that cautious look again. "I've been meaning to give you a call, but it's been really busy at the station. Haven't had time to myself."

Sharon turned to him from his other side. "Have you learned any more about the vet?" she asked.

I leaned forward to give her a dirty look. "He just got here, Sharon. He's not working," I said, and heard how abrupt I sounded.

John turned his head to look at me, chuckled and slid his arm along the back of my chair. "That's okay, Tee," he said softly, turning a little toward Sharon to answer her.

"There hasn't been anything new in the case," he said. "We're still working with the Coast Guard, hoping to find some wreckage of his boat. Something, anything to try to find what happened to him. So far nothing has come up."

"The other body, the one Tee found, that was the guy that was with him, right?"

"Yeah. We have nothing new on that either. We have to wait for the medical reports, just like the rest of you." He looked up as Greg returned and handed beers around the table.

He thanked him, lifted the bottle and took a long drink.

"What about Tee's assault? The guy that jumped her in the park?" Sharon asked.

I wanted to choke her, surprising myself with that thought, feeling my shoulders stiffen.

John turned his head to look directly into my eyes. He grinned down at me. "That appears to be an isolated incident, nothing directly related to Tee. No one saw anything but nothing else has happened, just a random incident, like her truck. String of bad luck. I'm going to be keeping an eye on her. She's going to be fine."

It sounded like a promise.

Sharon persisted. "Nothing on the guy in the park?"

"Nope. I went back over the past few months. No one has had a problem there. We have reports from last summer about guys asking for handouts, and a few drunk and disorderly arrests during the holidays."

"What do you think? As a police officer, I mean. Do you think he was after Tee?

"C'mon Sharon," I interrupted, "I really don't want to talk about this. Can we change the subject?"

"Oh, honey, I'm sorry," she said, reaching out and patting my hand. "I didn't mean to hog the conversation. Why don't you guys dance?"

She's really good at throwing me into awkward situations. I was thinking up a reply when John slid his chair back and offered his hand.

"Good idea," he said with a smile.

I stood up and let him lead me to the small dance floor, his hand warm around mine.

"Sorry about that," I said.

"Don't be," he said softly, pulling me into his arms.

I shyly put my hand on his shoulder and moved closer to him. Thank heavens it was a slow song. He was a very good dancer and I was trying to keep up, very aware of his arms around me, the warmth of his hand on my waist.

"Relax," he whispered, pulling me in a little closer. "Or are you still sore?"

"No, I'm good. How about you?"

"Oh, I was okay. Not my first wrestling match."

"At least you got the guy," I said.

He grinned down at me as we danced. "It's easier when you can see the guy, and you're bigger than he is. Not to mention I have a lot of experience. Seems like my whole career has involved taking guys down. It's no big deal, Tee."

"I'm really glad to have you across the street."

"I'm really glad to be there," he said, his eyes warm in the soft light.

We danced the following dance too, not talking much, just moving around the floor. It was easy to just be here with him, his arm around my waist, and the other hand warm around mine.

Several times he pulled his head back and looked at me, like he was deciding something. I could feel his gaze and blushing, I buried my head in his shoulder.

His arms tightened around me and he pulled me in closer.

He kept his hand at my waist as we rejoined the table, pulling out my chair, asking if I wanted another beer. To be fair he asked the whole table and took a couple of orders. It was getting late so I opted for coffee, as did several others.

"Be right back," John said, giving my shoulder a pat as left the table.

Sharon leaned over. "Wow. That's going well. He seems to like you," she grinned. "He fits in with the gang, too, even the Butcher, the Baker and the undertaker."

She was referring to Archie, who was indeed the butcher at the meat market, Cora, who owned our bakery, and Bill, who was not an undertaker although he could pass for one.

We all fondly referred to him as But Bill.

Every sentence he spoke had a negative qualifier attached, such as that dress is pretty but the color is wrong. She's nice and good looking but she never had an original thought. You get the idea. The wonder was that he never changed the habit. He had done it since high school.

John did fit well. He knew Arch from a previous case, asked intelligent questions of But Bill and complimented Cora on her shop. He even knew she was known for her pies, and admitted to peach being his favorite.

Cora supplied the diner with their pies, getting up an extra couple of hours early to bake and deliver them before opening her bakery.

He laughed at the jokes, seriously discussed the football scores, dividing his attention around the table like a dealer with a fresh deck.

Sharon was waggling her eyebrows at me so much I was afraid she would achieve lift off. In general she behaved like a fifteen year old at a sock hop.

"Stop it," I said, watching John at the bar, talking to a guy I didn't know but he obviously did. "I invited him, so it's not like he asked me out."

"Well, yes it is. He showed up, didn't he? And he stayed. I've been watching you two. He wants to be here, Tee. No one is twisting his arm." She patted my hand. "You two look good together."

He was soon back with a tray of cups and two carafes of coffee that he set in the middle of the table. He took two cups, putting one in front of me, and filled them before he sat back down.

"Good idea, coffee as the last round," he said to the table in general.

Greg laughed on the other side of the table. "It's been great to have you join us, John," he said, "but none of us has forgotten you're a cop. No one here is going to drive home unless they are completely sober."

John laughed with them, his face relaxing into a warm smile, as he put up a hand for a high five.

He looked so relaxed, so at ease with these people, some he had just met for the first time.

"I should get going," he said. "Are you okay to drive," he asked, turning once again to me, "or would you like a ride?"

"I'm fine, thanks," I said. "I can get home okay."

"You're sure? It's not like your place is out of my way." His dark eyes glinted in the dim light, a grin playing around his mouth.

Sharon turned to him. "It was nice to see you," she said, "I hope you'll join us again."

He smiled at her and stood up, pushing his chair back, replacing it at the table behind us. With his hand on my shoulder he leaned in close to me. "You can count on it. Thanks for the invitation. It was fun." I felt his lips brush my cheek.

"Sure," I said, smiling up at him, knowing I was blushing again and not caring.

He said his good nights to the table and ruffled my hair as he left.

I watched him go.

When he was out the door I sighed and turned back to the table. I looked up to see all eyes on me, the whole group grinning.

Oh, boy, here we go.

~~~

Saturday I was up and out early, hitting a lot of sales. I bought quilts and linens from the forties in very good condition, several bracelets, a complete set of Gibson dishes and, of course, three boxes of books.

The back of the Explorer was packed so I decided to take it all home and unload before joining Sharon for lunch. After six trips up and down the steps I didn't want anything but a cold Coke.

I filled a glass with ice, poured a Coke and sat down at the dining room table.

John's truck was gone again. Maybe he worked today.

I hoped he had enjoyed himself with my friends the night before, and wasn't just saying that to be polite. My mind wandered back over our small talk and chatter the previous evening. I remembered the feel of his arms when we danced, the soft brush of his lips on my cheek when he left.

I hoped I didn't imagine that part.

Taking my Coke with me I went back to my office and fired up the computer. While it booted I retrieved my backup camera from the new fanny pack and removed the memory card so I could load up the new pictures I had taken of the stuff I bought.

Meticulous records are necessary in any business and particularly in this one. The last thing I ever wanted was to find out I bought stolen property.

Sadly, that does get reported once in a while.

Books are safe bets. There's not enough money in used books to gain the interest of thieves, plus it's a long term gamble. A book may sit on the shelf for six months or longer before it sells. Or, it may never sell. Readers are among the most peculiar people on earth. I know. I'm one of them.

I was labeling my pictures prior to sending the copies to my online cloud when my cell phone rang.

I left it on the kitchen counter when I was pouring the Coke. I trotted to the kitchen and grabbed it, recognizing Sharon's number.

"You missed lunch," she said with a giggle, "something better come up?"

Sighing I sat down. "Just bought a lot today. Wanted to get it unloaded and on record. The time got away from me. I should have called. I'm sorry."

"No problem. Cora and Diane were here, still talking about your date last night."

"It was not a date, Sharon! He came by and had a couple of beers. With everyone, not just me."

"Uh-huh. And he made it quite clear that he was with you. He didn't dance with anyone else. Not to mention the way he looked at you."

"Oh, come on! It was not that bad. Besides, it was pretty noisy in there. He had to sit close to hear me."

"You tell yourself that, girl. You didn't see the way he was looking at you. I've seen that look on hungry dogs."

I could feel my cheeks warming up. This was worse than high school.

"And he's not home, smarty pants. His truck has been gone all day."

"Aha! Watching for him, are you?"

When I denied it, she started laughing. "Remember Randy Berry?"

I laughed along with her.

Randy was the captain of the football team in high school and we had worn out three pairs of shoes walking past his house on the off chance we might see him.

He didn't know either one of us. It was the 'what if' that kept us on our routine. The one and only time we saw him we burst into giggles and took off running.

"I can't really help it this time," I said. "The kitchen window faces his driveway."

She was stuck in remember when and talked for ten minutes about our high school adventures. When she finally got off the line, I refilled my Coke and went back to my office to finish up my inventory and load my pictures.

FLASH
Hey, Tim, where have you been?
Miss me, Muse?

Of course I did. I'm kind of used to having you to talk to at night.

You seem to be spending more time talking to the cop.

Because you're not here.

Nice move. So any news?

About what? The dead guy is still dead. The police are waiting on medical reports. Still no wreckage from the boat.

How about the guy that jumped you in the park?

Nothing there either. John says there's really nothing they can do with that one.

John? Kind of cozy now, huh?

You are being silly.

Me? You're the one hanging out with the guy.

How do you know?

Just a lucky guess.

What now? You read my mind?

Heck, no, I have other things to do. I just like to be sure you're okay. You're my inspiration, too. That's why I call you Muse. You're my muse. Where would I be if I lost you?

Uninspired?

Very. So you seeing more of the cop?

What's the problem with John?

I don't trust him. None of this stuff happened till you got in with him. I told you that. Several times.

Why on earth would a detective attack me?

Right back at ya. Why would anyone attack you? Why would someone break into your truck? That's what concerns me. You ask this guy for help, and things go south.

I think you're being too suspicious.

Then humor me. Be extra careful around this guy.

I am being extra careful around everyone I know.

And I'm being overly cautious, Muse. You've had a really rough couple of years. I don't want to see you in trouble again.

I'm fine, Tim, really. My two year tests are next month. If they're clear I have an excellent chance of beating cancer, that maybe it won't come back.

Then I'll feel better. Please, just be careful around this guy.

I will.

He was quiet for a few minutes.

I tried to open my mind, reach out to him.

Tim?

I wished for the hundredth time he would tell me when he was leaving. I often found myself blathering away with no response.

Most of the time I felt like Tim was my common sense, helping me pick the right path or the right thing to do. If that was true, was I warning myself? Using Tim as a sounding board?

When he failed to respond after a few more minutes, I gave up and went out to see what was available in the kitchen.

By the middle of the week I had sold books, the bracelets and a quilt for a tidy profit. Packaging everything up I took it to the post office and shipped it out.

The post office is across the street from Kelly's small parking lot. I looked over to see if Sharon's car was in the lot, but guessed I had missed her, since I didn't see it.

I left my truck parked in front of the post office and jogged across the street.

"Jaywalking! That's a fine," called a voice I recognized.

John was just pulling into the lot. He shook a finger at me, shaking his head, then parked in a slot. I waited on the sidewalk for him to join me.

"Do I get a ticket?" I called as he jogged across the street and joined me.

He was in jeans and a long sleeved shirt, with the sleeves rolled up, so I didn't know if he was off duty or working.

Come to think of it, I never saw him in a uniform.

He threw an arm around my shoulders, pulled me to his side in a hug, then opened the door to Kelly's and held it for me.

"Only a warning this time, sweetheart, next time it's off to jail."

"I am forewarned," I said, stopping inside the door to look for Sharon.

"Meeting someone?" he asked.

"Just looking for Sharon. We hook up a couple of times a week but I'm running late today. I don't see her."

He took my elbow. "Come on then, I can use the company. I'll even buy."

He guided me to an open booth and then slid in across from me. "I'm going to assume you don't need a menu."

I laughed. "I think anyone who has lived here more than a month knows the menu by heart. It's still the best food around and you can't beat the price."

"Monarch is pretty casual about everything. Kelly's is breakfast and lunch, the Gem for pizza and beer. Where do you go for a date?" John looked sincerely interested. He had been here for over a year. He should know by now.

"You've been here long enough to figure that one out," I said. "If you want expensive and elegant it's Hill House. If you want classy and great food, it's Tahlia's. If you just want to impress someone with ambiance, it's the Bayside Country Club in San Luis."

I had forgotten to grab a cup so I fiddled with my napkin and spoon.

"Okay," he nodded. "If you, personally, were going on a date, where would you go?"

I smiled at him. "Truthfully? There's no one I want to impress enough to buy a dress for Hill House. The Gem is fine for pizza and hanging out with the gang, and," I gestured at our surroundings, "this is good the rest of the time. I get take out from here for supper all the time. As you know, I sometimes order from Thalia's and take it home. So asking me where I would go on a date? No good answer."

"Then I assume you don't have a special someone?"

I rearranged my silverware, not looking at him.

"Not really," I finally said. "All my friends are special to me." I finally looked him in the eye. "To be honest, I think I like it that way."

"You think? Not sure?"

"My life has been kind of squirrelly the last couple of years. I'm happy to be where I am"

"I know you had cancer. Are you still in treatment for that?" He looked serious, leaning on his elbows, paying close attention.

"Nope, two years coming up. I have to have a PET scan next month that will mark my two year anniversary. My doctors say that if I get to three years, I have a good

123

chance of beating it. They count from your diagnosis, so right now I am closing in on two years without cancer."

He reached over and took my hand, giving my fingers a squeeze before letting go.

"I'm sure you're okay," he smiled. "At least I hope so."

"Me, too. I hope I never have to go through that again. How about you? Every single gal in Monarch Beach wants to know your story. Why don't you have a special someone?"

He sat back again. "To tell you the truth, without all the gory details, I'm the guy who came home and found his wife in bed with his best friend. The best lesson I learned from that experience is that I don't want to be the guy in bed with someone else's wife, or girlfriend. How about you?"

"Only me," I answered. "And the cats."

I could claim Tim but that was going to take a lot of explaining.

Sally was sauntering over with her order pad.

"Hi Sally," I smiled.

John glanced behind him, saw her and straightened up. "What's good today, sweetheart?" he greeted her.

I noted the endearment. Did he call all women sweetheart? I was pretty sure that was not politically correct.

"Everything," she said. "Although we're out of peach pie already. You're going to have to settle for apple or pumpkin."

He turned his smile on me. "See how well she knows me? This lady knows what I like."

"Does that mean you want fish and chips again?"

This time he laughed. "Yes, Sally, I believe I do. Side salad, please, ma'am and iced tea. Not sure what time I'll get to dinner so I don't want to leave hungry."

She squirmed like a friendly pup under his gaze. "How about you, Tee?

"Cobb salad."

"Dressing on the side."

I looked at John. "She knows all of us," I grinned. "Yes, ma'am and bleu cheese dressing please."

Sally made a note then looked at John. "The only thing that changes with her is the dressing. You might want to remember that for the future."

"What is that supposed to mean?" I asked.

"Just what I said, sugar. The only thing that changes with you is the dressing. That means you are very predictable and very set in your ways. Maybe you should break lose once in a while, kick up your heels a little."

"Order the cole slaw," John threw in, "just to irritate her."

Sally slapped her fanny suggestively and left us to place our orders.

"Are you really that set in your ways?" He asked when she was out of hearing range.

"I don't think so," I said truthfully. "Chemo and brain radiation both affect memory, so mine is a little faulty at times. It's getting better," I hastened to add. "To help with that I have routines, doing things in a certain order, repeating them. It helps my memory."

"Being orderly is a good thing, sign of an organized person."

Sally ambled up with John's iced tea. "Organization is for wimps," she said.

"I'm a wimp, then," I said.

"I'm teasing you, sweetie," she said, "I think you're amazing to do what you do. I can remember when you had trouble holding your head up long enough to open the front door." She patted my shoulder. "We're all proud of you, Tee. That was a tough time."

"And I would prefer to forget it," I said.

"Got it," she said, and left without another word.

"Sensitive subject?"

I sighed. "Not really. It's the past, it's gone. People mean well. It's the constant reminder. You know? I still have to be tested, every three to six months, different tests, different doctors, so it's always on my mind. I had the kind of cancer that comes back. I know that. My doctors know that, that's why the tests. It gets to be enough, you know?"

"I can see where it would. I won't mention it again."

"That's okay," I smiled. "You don't know if you don't ask."

"Exactly," he smiled. "That's why I asked if you were involved with someone."

Back where we started. Am I involved with someone? Do I want to be?

With a deep breath I said, "I am not involved with anyone. I was married, it didn't work so I've been alone most of my life. I've been through the whole cancer thing. There were a couple of times I didn't know if I was going to make it and there were times I didn't care one way or the other. Now things are looking up. I have a place to live, my online business, a couple of bookkeeping clients, the rentals and the cats." I looked at him. "I don't know if I have the time, or the energy, to give to someone."

Sally was approaching with our plates so we both straightened silverware and napkins, making room.

When the plates were delivered she went back to the kitchen, leaving us without her usual remarks.

I picked up the pepper while John took the salt.

It didn't seem like the right time to ask about the vet's case, so we settled into small talk and chatted amiably over our late lunches, mostly about books. He repeated his intention to visit my bookcases.

I scanned the customers several times but never did see Sharon. I made a mental note to give her a call when I got home.

I also caught several people staring at us while we ate. They looked away when I caught them at it.

When we were finished John paid the tab and walked out with me. On the sidewalk, he pointed at my truck across the street.

"Use the crosswalk, ma'am. No more jaywalking." He gave me a very public hug on the sidewalk, in front of Kelly's windows, folding me in with both arms. He kept an arm around my shoulders as he walked me to the corner.

He escorted me to my truck, held the door for me, and closed it behind me. With a one finger salute he walked around my truck and headed for the police station.

I went to the market to do some grocery shopping. I was sure the boys would appreciate it since cat food topped the list.

Settled in that night with Cletus on one side and Dave on the other, I found my mind wandering from my current read on the Kindle.

Thinking about what John had said this afternoon, I wondered. Did I want someone else in my life? More important, was I willing to give the time and energy it takes to have a relationship?

The past two years there had been no room to even consider anyone else, except doctors and nurses. Now that I was on the upswing, getting back on my feet and enjoying it, did I really want to give up time to another person?

Admittedly it was flattering to have the attention of a good looking man. He had put us both in the spotlight with his attention lately.

We had a lot of similar interests. He was bright and funny and I enjoyed his company. There's also the old ego thing, you know? While the other single gals in town are scheming and plotting, the prize falls into my lap.

Did I want the prize?

That was the question.

Granted, I enjoyed his company, and the attention. On the other hand, if we were involved, it could escalate to a more intimate relationship. Was I ready for that?

And maybe I was jumping the gun. Maybe John wanted someone share a meal once in a while. I may have read too much into what he said. It might be nice to have someone to eat dinner with a couple of times a week, someone to talk to, besides Tim.

And how would John feel about sharing me with a mental companion that he couldn't see or hear? Was I ready to explain Tim? Then there was the reverse. How would Tim feel? He had seemed a little annoyed about me spending time with John.

One thing I knew for sure. Tim had been there for me, gone through a lot with me. I was not about to give him up. Not for anyone.

Round and round it went, what if this and what if that. I had no idea what I had read. I turned off the Kindle and laid it aside. The cats were curled up and settled for the night. I joined them.

Like Scarlett, I'd worry about it tomorrow.

The sales on Saturday were slim. I picked up a few books and finished by ten. I got to Kelly's before Sharon, picked up a cup and snagged her favorite booth.

"Any news?" Sally asked, filling my cup.

"Sally, you have more information than I ever will. You tell me. What's happening?"

Sally smirked at the compliment, glanced around and slid into the booth across from me.

"Well," she lowered her voice, "the results of the autopsy are in. The body you found didn't drown. He was killed by a blow to the back of the head." She sat back. "They finally found some debris from the boat washing around at Jade Cove. There's a team working there now. The Coast Guard is back, cruising around, so maybe this time they'll find where it went down."

She lumbered back to her feet with a sigh, picked up the coffee carafe and leaned down. "I would think that you would know more than I do, since you're the one dating the lead detective."

I knew this was coming.

I motioned her closer and she bent her head.

"John and I are neighbors," I said. "We can't help but see each other."

"You've been neighbors for over a year and never went dancing," she grinned. "And everyone here saw him hug you when you left the other day." She folded her arms and looked at me.

"Okay, here's the scoop, between you and me. I've had supper with my neighbor, John, a couple of times. We ran into each other at the Gem and danced a few times."I leaned in closer to Sally and dropped my voice. "If anything else happens you will be the first to know." I sat back and grinned at her.

"Ok, sweetie, I'm gonna hold you to that." And off she went.

I returned to the paper when a shadow fell across the table. Expecting Sharon, I sat up and leaned back to find John standing there.

"Want some company?" Without waiting for an answer he slid in across from me.

"Sure," I said. "I didn't see you come in."

"I saw you come in," he grinned. "What are you having?"

"Fried chicken. I can never eat it all so I get two meals out of it. Take home the leftovers and warm them up for supper."

"Sounds good to me. Order me the same, with iced tea," he slid out of the booth. "I want to wash up."

He headed to the back where the restrooms were.

Sally brought my salad and iced tea, looking around. "Didn't I see that good looking man with you?"

"He's washing up. He wants the fried chicken," I answered.

She pulled out her order pad. "Same check?"

"Sure, why not."

"Iced tea for him too?"

"Yes, ma'am."

"What kind of dressing on the salad?"

Phooey. "Ranch?"

"He usually gets Italian," she smirked.

"Then make it Italian," I sighed.

With a swish she turned and headed for the kitchen at almost the same time John came back and took his place across the table.

"So how was your day?" he asked, hands folded in front of him. "Anything exciting happen?"

"No, thank heavens. Nice quiet week."

"Good. Glad to hear it."

"Me, too. How about you? Any news on the boat? Sally said the Coast Guard was cruising Jade Cove."

"Yeah, they're back. A couple of surfers reported stuff floating in the Cove so we have a team over there checking on it, trying to get it up on the beach. Doesn't mean it's from the Witch. That all has to be sorted out. It's something, though."

"Witch?"

"Name of the boat. Sea Witch."

"Oh, I hope it is," I said. "Mildred is getting her check soon. I know she'd like to have some closure before she leaves." I shuddered. "I know I would never want to see the ocean again if it was me."

Sally brought his tea and salad, took extra time delivering his silver ware.

"Any news from the Cove?"

He grinned at her, moving his hands to make room for the salad. "You'll know before I do," he said. "You always do."

I swear she simpered, if I knew what simpered looked like.

"Thanks, sweetheart," he said, digging into the salad. "I'm really hungry tonight."

"Oh, you're always hungry," she giggled, patting his shoulder, trailing her fingers along his arm. She finally wandered back toward the kitchen.

"I think she has a crush," I said, adding pepper to my own salad.

"She's a sweetie, one of my best informants."

"She's an informant? Really?"

"You think you're the only one who takes advantage of the gossip?"

"I don't take advantage of it," I said, "I just listen to it. I'd miss a lot of really good sales if it wasn't for her and Sharon."

"See? She's a hot bed of information. We all depend on Sally to tell us what's happening."

Our orders arrived. We both took time to arrange napkins, add salt and pepper, all the little prenuptials we go through in preparation of eating.

We were still fiddling with our plates when Sally was back with refills on the iced tea.

"Anything else I can get you folks?"

"We're good," John told her, picking up a chicken leg.

"I know that, darlin'." She smiled at him and went to fill someone else's tea glass.

We both dug into our food and conversation dropped to "pass the salt" and "more butter?"

I liked that. I didn't have to worry about small talk. When we finally sat back, wiping our faces and fingers, we smiled across the table.

"Can't beat the food," John said with a sigh.

"Got that right," I agreed, "and enough chicken left for supper."

"Do you want this too?" he asked, indicating his last piece of chicken.

"No, thanks, you should save it, take it home. It won't go to waste."

"Good idea. I get hungry when I read."

I chuckled at him. "I used to fix a plate of snacks before I opened the book."

"No more?"

"Nope. Now it's just me and my Kindle."

That launched a ten minute discussion on e-readers versus regular books, during which Sally boxed up leftovers and left them on the table.

I picked up the check before John could reach it. "My turn."

He grinned at me but didn't argue. Sliding out of the booth he folded a tip and stuck it under the edge of his plate.

"You headed home now?" he asked. "Or to the Gem? It's Saturday night."

"I think I'm going to make it an early night," I said.

"I'll buy you a beer," he said, giving me a long look from under his lashes. "Come on. I can't be out late. I have to be up early."

His eyes had that little gleam that hinted at something more. I didn't have anything to do really, and I still hadn't seen Sharon this week.

"One beer."

"Good deal, meet you there," he grinned. "I gotta get back to work."

"See you later." I stood up and picked up my box of leftovers.

He let me precede him to the cash register, offering no argument when I paid.

We parted on the sidewalk with a wave, going in different directions.

I headed home, a little eager for tonight.

Chapter Seven

The parking lot was more than half full when I got to the Gem. I drove around to the back and found a spot under the lights. Making sure I locked my truck I went around the building to the front, watching for John's truck.

A silver pickup pulled in and went to the right, looking for a spot up front. I wasn't sure it was John but it looked like his truck.

There were certainly a lot of silver pickups around. Seems like I saw one every time I left the house. Or is this a new aberration from a disturbed mind? Tim had been missing for a few days. Maybe I was trading him in for an obsession with silver pickups?

My bunch had the corner table as usual, so I made my way over, waving to others I knew. Archie pulled a chair out for me and I sat down next to Sharon.

"Hey, stranger," I greeted her, giving her a brief hug. "Where have you been? Everything okay?"

She returned the hug, then smiled at me. "Oh, I've been around. You've just been too busy to notice."

"What do you mean?"

"I was at Kelly's today, just got there a little later than usual. You were all snuggled in with John Kincaid."

"You could have joined us," I said. "We ran into each other, it wasn't planned."

"Uh - huh. You two looked so cozy, laughing and talking, I didn't want to interrupt."

"You would not have interrupted," I insisted. "We were only having lunch."

"And is he meeting you here?" Her green eyes danced.

"Do you want a beer?" I felt my cheeks getting warm.

She laughed. "Yes, I do, and I will even buy you one to make up for the teasing." She waved at the bar and held up two fingers, then slid her chair out and leaned over for another hug. "I think it's great, sweetie."

When she came back, we clicked bottles and started catching up.

Sharon is a single mom with twin girls in college, so she always has news or stories to tell. I hadn't seen the girls in a while so she had a lot to update. I am an honorary Aunt to Melanie and Marsha.

While we talked I kept an eye on the front door, watching for John.

Archie bought a round for the table and we were half way through those when John finally showed up.

"Sorry, sweetheart," he said, sliding a chair in next to me. "I got stuck at the station and I have to go back. Something came up."

"No problem," I smiled, although I was disappointed.

"One of the perks of the job," he grinned. "One the academy doesn't teach. Like doctors and firemen, never know when you may be called. I just wanted to let you know. In person."

He kissed my cheek quickly then stood up and pushed in the chair. "I'll make it up to you," he winked. "Sharon, good to see you, even for a minute."

136

He waved to Archie and Cora and made his apologies. "Next week first round is on me," he called as he made his way back to the door.

Sharon patted my hand. "Hey, at least he came by and let you know."

"Oh, I'm fine. He can't help it, it's his job. Besides, it was spur of the minute, no big deal."

"It is a big deal," she said. "No one likes to be stood up. Don't give up on it, okay? Things just happen."

We've been friends for a long time, since the crib, and I knew she had my best interests at heart. Of course my feelings were hurt although he had stopped by long enough to let me know.

My doubt was whether I really wanted to be this involved, to let someone else's presence control my moods, my feelings. It's one thing to flirt, another to become involved.

I liked the flutter of attention. Hey, I'm human and he's a good looking man.

On the other hand, relationships take a lot of work. Like a bank account, you can't take out more than you put in. I'd been through a lot this past year, getting my feet under me.

Did I really want another change? One that could be very complicated emotionally?

Pride demanded I stay a little longer, unwilling to give my friends any more to talk about.

Standing rule in Monarch: you are either present or you are the subject. I knew I had been the subject for the last week or so. I did not want to throw another log on that fire.

I stuck it out another hour and then made my escape, promising Sharon we'd have brunch tomorrow for sure.

Although I knew there were two pieces of fried chicken in the fridge I decided a chili dog would taste better, so I drove up to the drive thru by the freeway and ordered a couple of chili dogs. With onions. Right? A bonus to having no significant other.

Driving back home I nibbled on the fries while driving with one hand. I hate to get grease on the steering wheel.

I was making the turn onto my street when yet another big silver pickup dang near hit me, doing more than the speed limit for our neighborhood. I thought it was John but he was moving too fast to be sure.

I hoped everything was okay, seeing him speed off like that. I made a quick right to pull into the drive, then a quick left into my driveway. I put on the brake, grabbed my food, and climbed out of the truck pushing the auto lock before I shut the door.

I rounded the corner of the house and stopped.

The front yard was dark.

I was sure I turned on the porch light when I left.

Coming around the front I saw something move on the front porch, back in the shadows near the front door.

Something, a shade lighter than the shadows, had moved.

Jumping back around the corner I looked to see if John's lights were on, then remembered he was working tonight.

I retreated and set the bag of food on top of the truck. I moved out to the drive, putting space between me and my house, working my way along the drive until I was out in the main driveway.

Now, I had a clear view of the front porch.

Without the porch light on it was hard to see details in the shadows. I was sure I had left it on. Maybe the bulb had burned out. I couldn't see squat in the dark.

Then that lighter spot moved. And meowed.

"Dave?"

He meowed again and came to the steps where I could almost make out his shape.

I hurried across the yard, calling him as I went so I didn't scare him.

He had never been outside, not in the time I had him. I talked softly to him as I got nearer to the steps, afraid he would bolt left or right and be lost in the dark.

He waited for me, complaining quite vocally.

When I got within reach I scooped him up, grateful he didn't fight me, and backed carefully down the steps.

I made it to my truck, opened the door and sat Dave on the front seat. I was climbing in to join him when I heard another cry, a forlorn yowl. From the front porch.

Cletus.

How did the cats get outside?

There was only one way.

Someone had let them out.

Someone who might still be inside.

Easing the door shut on the truck, with Dave inside, I pulled out my cell and dialed 911. I tried to explain the situation, not sure if someone was in the house or not and asking for assistance.

There was no way I was going in alone.

The guy on the line told me to stay in the truck and lock the doors, help was on the way.

Hearing my voice set Cletus off and he yowled again.

How could I leave him alone out there? He had to be terrified. Dave picked up the call and started meowing back from the truck.

I moved as quickly and quietly as I could back to the front steps, calling softly for Cletus.

He wasn't on the steps. I moved up the steps, one at a time, clicking my tongue at him.

Finally I saw a lighter patch in a corner near the front door. He crouched against the boards, his eyes huge even in the dark of the porch.

"Cletus?" I whispered, "Come on, baby boy." I held my hand out to him, knowing there was no way he would allow me to pick him up.

He crept forward, away from the door, and sniffed my fingers. I talked baby talk to him, slowly moving my hand to scratch his ears, stroke his back.

He was shaking like he was cold, his whole body trembling.

I backed away a couple of steps, still talking softly to him and slowly peeled off my shirt. Holding it in one hand, I got down on my hands and knees, creeping back up the steps, still talking to him.

I coaxed Cletus down to the second step, where I could reach out and pet him. I spent several minutes petting him and talking to him, sliding the shirt up closer to him.

He stiffened a couple of times like he was going to bolt but stayed put, stretching his neck out to sniff the shirt.

With a deep breath I threw the shirt over him, lurched up and grabbed him, bundling him tightly in my shirt and holding him against my chest.

At the same time I scurried away, back towards the truck where Dave was still yowling loud enough to wake the dead.

When I reached the truck I popped the locks open with the keyless entry and climbed quickly into the front seat before Dave could bolt out.

Once inside I released Cletus, who clawed his way under the front seat. Dave jumped from the seat back to the floor and sniffed his brother, now hidden under the seat.

A sweep of light lit up the truck and I heard a car door slam.

I looked and saw the black and white squad car in the street.

Careful of the cats, I cracked the door open again and slipped out before the cats could escape.

Out of the truck I ran for the officer getting out of the car. The light from his flashlight hit me full in the face.

"Put your hands on top of your head," he ordered, keeping the light in my face.

I raised my hands. "I'm the one who called," I told him, "This is my house. I have ID in my back pocket."

Thankfully he dropped the light a little lower and stepped closer.

"Keep your hands on your head and turn around slowly," he instructed.

I did what he said.

"My ID is in a card case in my right rear pocket," I said.

"Remove it slowly, please, and hand it over."

I pulled my card case out and held it to the side where he could see that was all I had in my hand. Holding it with thumb and forefinger, I turned slightly to hand it back to him. I felt him take it out of my fingers.

"Can I lower my arms?" I asked.

"Yes, ma'am," he said, lowering the light to the ground and stepping up to return my identification. "I'm sorry for the inconvenience. I had to be sure you were the reporting party. Do you have a jacket or a shirt?"

Belatedly I realized I'm out here in my jeans and bra, having used my shirt to capture Cletus.

"My clothes are inside." I led the way to the front porch, pulling my keys out of my pocket.

"What seems to be the problem?" He asked, following me up the steps to the front door.

"I just got home and I think someone may be in my house. I found my cats outside, and they never go outside. The porch light is out, and I'm pretty sure I left it on."

"Just a minute," he said, stepping in and taking my keys. "Please stand back, ma'am. If you'll just wait on the grass," he ordered, then said something into his shoulder mike and followed me down the steps.

"Another car is coming, ma'am. If you'll just wait in your truck or on the lawn, we'll check the residence for you."

I nodded and backed up to my truck.

Looking inside there was no sign of either cat. I opened the door slowly, then jumped in and shut it quickly. Turning in the seat I got on my knees and felt around in the back for my tee shirt.

I finally found it and pulled it on. Being dressed I felt a little better and a little less stupid.

Within minutes another squad car pulled up, followed by a big silver pickup that pulled into the parking space across the drive. This time it was the right truck.

John got out, waved to me and jogged over to join the two cops.

They spoke for a few minutes. I couldn't hear what they were saying so I lowered the window a couple of inches, not enough for a quick cat to escape. I hoped to hear what was happening.

The three of them trooped out of sight, towards the porch.

There was nothing for a few minutes, then the porch light flashed on, lighting the front yard.

John came around the corner and walked toward me, silhouetted against the now bright lawn.

I got out of the truck, again taking care to shut the door without squashing a cat, and met him at the edge of the drive.

"The guys are checking your place, now. What happened?" he asked when he was close.

I explained what I had seen, the cats out, catching them and getting them into the truck. I didn't mention that I was wandering around in the yard without a shirt when the first officer showed up.

"You didn't go inside?"

"No."

"All right. You're okay?

I nodded.

"Stay in the truck, and keep the doors locked. I'll go see what's going on inside. Then I'll come back and let you know."

He went back around to the front while I climbed yet again into the truck. With a sigh, I leaned my head against the head rest and closed my eyes.

It seemed like hours before I heard them coming back out on the porch.

I sat up.

Easing out of the truck again I made my way around front.

All three men stood on the fully lighted porch. The front door was open and a lamp in my living room glowed behind them.

One of the officers was writing on a clipboard. They talked so softly I couldn't hear what was being said. I edged up closer to the porch, shivering in the cool night.

When John saw me at the foot of the steps he dismissed the other two cops. They both touched their caps as they left.

I watched them get in their squad cars, back out, and leave. John came down the steps and folded me into his arms.

For a couple of minutes he just held me, rocking me gently, like a child. I curled into his arms, laid my head on his broad chest and closed my eyes.

"I need you to see if anything is missing," he finally said, stepping back but keeping one arm around me. "It's a mess but no permanent damage. Just be prepared," he warned.

I moved around him, his hand on my waist and went into the living room.

It looked like a tornado had blown through the whole house.

It's creepy to know someone has been in your home, to realize that some strange person has been in your space, touched your stuff, and prowled around uninvited.

Goose bumps rose on my arms as I looked around my home.

Books were all over the floor, both bookcases emptied and dumped. The magazines that had been on the end table were strewn everywhere, some pages torn, and bits of paper like confetti covering the carpet.

The boxes left on the dining room table were dumped, tossed around the floor. Broken glass glittered among the pages and papers.

The kitchen was the worst. All the cabinets were opened and emptied all over the floor. The smells of coffee and cinnamon hung heavy in the air.

I stepped carefully into the room and looked at the mess, tears welling up in my eyes. I crunched my way to the back porch, following a draft of air.

Glass covered my laundry room floor, glass shards that had previously been the window in my back door glittered in the laundry soap dumped on the floor. The light breeze coming in through the broken window fluttered dryer sheets thrown on the floor.

Why?

I turned and went back across the dining room to the corner I used as my office.

It had suffered the same fate, shelves dumped and books everywhere. My carefully arranged files were scattered about, the drawers of my desk pulled out and dumped, sheets of paper everywhere.

"I'm sorry," John said behind me. "I have to ask. Can you tell if anything is missing?"

"In this mess? I have no idea." I shrugged and turned to face him. "I keep pretty good records of everything. I should be able to tell if anything is gone in a day or so. It's going to take that long to clean this up. What about upstairs?" I pushed past him, back into the living room, headed to the stairs.

"It's the same." He followed me as I made my way upstairs.

Dresser drawers were dumped and thrown everywhere. Underwear, tee shirts, and socks covered the floor. More books tossed around, the bed stripped of its covers, the mattress half off the box spring.

The guest room and the bathroom matched the rest of the decor. In the hall, even the linen closet had been emptied, towels and sheets, pillowcases and wash cloths thrown everywhere.

I couldn't look at it any more.

I shoved John out of the way and almost ran down the stairs, back to the mess that had been my office. Taking a deep breath I tried to be objective, trying to reorganize it in my mind the way it had been.

"The computer," I said aloud, hearing John move up behind me.

"Anything else?"

Shaking my head I kept looking around. This room seemed to have gotten the worst of it. Books, papers, CD's all over the floor. "The computer is gone. Box of compact discs, about the size of a shoe box." I spread my hands about a foot apart.

"Was anything valuable on those?"

"Define valuable," I snapped. "My medical records, my tax records, Payroll records for my two clients, their

146

tax records. Lots of old songs. I listened to those when I was working."

I picked up some files and tried to stack them into some kind of pile and then I stopped. I couldn't look at it any more.

I pushed my way past John again and ran out the front door.

Outside, I stopped, bent over and put my hands on my knees, trying to take deep breaths. Waves of nausea washed over me. The tears started and I knew if I let go, I would not stop crying.

It was all too much.

I wondered idly if this was punishment for surviving cancer, some kind of karmic retribution. Survival guilt takes many forms.

After a few more minutes I wiped my eyes on my sleeve and straightened up.

John stood in the front door, arms folded, watching, waiting for me to gain control of myself.

From the truck I could hear the cats yowling, one or both of them. They must be terrified. I had to get to them.

"Anything else? I hate to do this to you, sweetheart, but I have to get a report filed. Is there anything of value you can think of, anything that could be sold or pawned?"

"Not that I can see," I said. "The computer is an older one, not worth much. The discs are personal, nothing of value. The only thing of any current value would be the television, and it's still here. The rest of it, not worth that much, certainly not worth pawning. It just looks like a huge mess to me."

"Did you remember to lock up when you left?"

I wanted to smack him, just double up my fist and hit him as hard as I could. Not a smart move with the investigating officer. I sighed again.

"Yes, I double checked both doors. I assume the broken window in the back door is how they got in?"

"It looks that way, hard to tell really. Nothing else jumps out at you? Nothing else missing?"

"I can't tell," I sighed. "Right now, I just want the cat food."

I went back in, made my way across to the kitchen and started sorting through the mess, trying to find the bag of dry cat food. Wonder of wonders half of it was still in the bag.

I picked a couple of undamaged bowls out of the litter and a bottle of water.

"For now I just want to feed my cats," I said. "The rest of it can wait till tomorrow. I can't do it tonight."

On my way back through the living room, I snagged the afghan from under the coffee table and carried it with me to the truck. Setting down the cats supplies, I shook the afghan out on the grass.

When I was pretty sure there was nothing harmful stuck to it, I bundled it up and stuck it under my arm.

Dave stood in the front seat, peering out the driver's side window, vocalizing his displeasure.

No sign of Cletus.

Using the remote from my keys I unlocked the back gate of the truck, tossed the afghan, cat food, water and bowls inside through the rear window, then shut it again before Dave could get to me.

The one bright spot was the back seat was already flat since I used it mostly for hauling boxes. I rarely had the back seat upright. Dave was quickly over the front seat, sniffing the bag of cat food.

John had followed me outside and now stood there, beside the truck, watching.

"You can stay with me tonight," he said softly. "I have a spare room. And tomorrow I can give you a hand putting things back in order."

He stepped forward and reached for me.

I stepped back, holding up a hand. "No offense, but I want to stay here, with the boys."

"In the truck? That's silly! There's a perfectly good bed forty feet from here." He reached out to take my hand. "It will look better in the morning."

Freeing my hand I stepped back again, bumped up against my truck. "Sorry, John. I appreciate it. I really do. The boys are scared and hungry. If you don't want to listen to them all night, I'm going to have to stay with them."

"We can board up the back window, so they can't get back out. I probably have some kind of boards that will work for tonight. They'll be okay back in the house."

Shaking my head, I moved back to the passenger door.

"Nope, thanks. I'll stay here."

"Fine," he said, and I could hear the anger in his voice, "suit yourself."

He mumbled something else I didn't hear, and was probably glad I didn't, then went back around to the front. "I'll lock up the front for you," he called back over his shoulder.

I wondered why. Why bother with it now?

I didn't even watch to see if he went home or back to the station.

Dave was busy pawing the cat food bag. I yanked the side door open quickly and climbed inside.

Dave rushed to me, purring and rubbing all over me - my arms, my leg, anything he could reach. His purr is very loud and now it filled the small space.

"It's okay, Davy," I said, stroking him.

I filled a bowl with cat food, then filled the other with water from the bottle. The yellow cat immediately starting lapping up water, looking up frequently to be sure I was still there.

I talked softly, kept petting him, and took comfort from his presence.

I was lucky they stayed on the porch. Having never been outside they could have taken off on a grand adventure. I could have lost them forever.

Tears filled my eyes again while I sat hunched over in the back, stroking the cat.

When he quit drinking, he turned to me and crawled up in my lap, sniffed my chin, rubbed against my arms. Purring, he curled up and began to wash his feet.

Reaching over him I pulled the afghan up and wrapped it around both of us, scooting down until I could mostly stretch out without spilling cat food or water.

Dave snuggled in beside me, still purring. His song and my tears lulled me to sleep.

~~~

I woke up at daybreak, surprised to find Dave still tucked up next to me and Cletus curled up behind my knees. There was no way to move without disturbing them and no way could I continue to lay on my hip.

Petting Cletus all the time, I slowly turned onto my back. Dave voiced his displeasure, then climbed on top of me and licked my chin.

My hip hurt, my back was stiff and my knees creaked when I tried to straighten them a little bit.

The sky was getting lighter by the minute. I could think of a thousand things I'd rather do than face the disaster that used to be my home.

Dave got down. He began to sniff around the back corner of the bay, pulling at a corner of the carpet with one paw.

"Hang on, Davy," I said, sitting up, my mind racing. If I pulled their litter box from the laundry room into the kitchen I could shut the door and keep the cats out of the glass and away from the open window.

Another thing I learned through the lethargy of chemo, is one step at a time.

I managed to get out of the truck, with a lot of snap, crackle and pop in my joints. Stretching my legs, I bent over and stretched out my back, too.

Going around to the front of the house I pulled out my keys and opened the door.

I didn't even look at the destruction of my neat and orderly existence, just shuffled my way through to the back.

I shoved the litter box inside the kitchen and closed off the laundry room, to keep the cats from getting back outside. The broken glass on the floor was mostly from the window and now contained to the laundry room.

I used my feet to kick a clear path through the mess of spices, condiments, dishes and silverware and go outside to retrieve the cats.

Dave was standing on the arm rest, waiting, so he was first. I knew he wouldn't be any trouble. I scooped him up and hopped out, closing the door behind me. I couldn't see Cletus.

Hurrying to the front door, I opened it just enough to shove Davy through and close it behind him.

Back at the truck, I opened the driver's door and got in, shutting the door behind me.

I called Cletus several times, talking softly to him, telling him my frustrations, my fears, anything that came to mind. Cat crap has a strong odor and I was happy enough not to smell it as I sat and talked.

I know I must have looked odd sitting in the truck in my drive and talking to myself, first thing in the morning, but what the heck? I'm a survivor. I don't give a fig how I look to others.

It took almost ten minutes but eventually the big yellow cat eased out from under the front seat and jumped up beside me, settling himself on the afghan I had folded. It was just minutes more to wrap him in it, cover his head, get out of the truck, and trot to the front door.

The cat was so frightened he froze in my arms, making it easy to get him inside.

When I got him in the house and released him, he didn't even run or hide. He sat down, looked up at me with those big yellow eyes, hoisted his back leg in the air and began his morning bath.

Perhaps we had bonded during last night's experience.

That thought cheered me a little as I went to face the kitchen. Cletus followed along and quickly joined Dave in a game of floor hockey, batting around the condiments, spices and packets on the floor.

Glancing out the kitchen window I saw that John's truck was not in evidence. So much for help.

With a sigh, I tore off a trash bag and got out the broom.

One step at a time, I told myself, one step at a time.

A couple of hours later the kitchen was taking shape. I could see the floor.

Answering a knock at the front door, I found Sharon and Cora loaded with coffee, donuts and bagels. Sharon set tall paper cups of coffee on the dining room table, left again, and returned with a cardboard box of cleaning supplies, rolls of trash bags, and a bright yellow scarf that she used to tie up her hair.

Stepping back to let them in I noticed John's truck was still absent.

Cora gave me a hug and handed me fresh coffee and a chocolate donut. "Everything is better with chocolate," she said, offering a napkin. "Take a break and get some sugar in your system. You need the energy."

The three of us sat at the table, eating donuts and drinking coffee while I filled them in on last night.

"All they took was the computer?" Sharon asked, wiping her fingers. "It wasn't even that new. What's the point? Just random violence?"

Cora leaned her elbows on the table. "Honey, I have to ask," she said. "Who the heck did you piss off? Everything that has happened to you has a personal feel to it. You know what I mean? Your truck, the park and now

153

this. For what? Pure meanness? Okay, you lost your camera but was that worth the risk? Someone will go to jail for that stunt, if they catch him, and I hope they do."

She sat back, having spoken her mind. Cora was usually taciturn. I don't think I ever heard her say that many words at one time. The fact that she voiced the same ideas as Tim didn't escape me.

"She's right," added Sharon. "You made someone mad. This," she waved a hand at the kitchen, "is pure vandalism. So was the truck."

"I agree," I said, "I just can't imagine what I did! You know me, Sharon. I mind my own business, and my business is in my home. I pay my bills on time. I meet my client's deadlines early. I have wracked my brain trying to figure out what I could have done to make someone this angry. Let's face it, I don't see that many people."

Sharon sighed. "I can't think of a thing. What about your online business? Could you have sold someone a fake? Made a mistake on a collectible book?"

"I can't see how and it wouldn't matter. Everything I sell can be returned for a full refund. If I did make a mistake, they could just email me and return it. Besides, how would they know where I live? What kind of truck I drive?"

"Return address?"

"Post Office box," I said. "I have been very careful to keep that information private."

"Was there anything in your truck? When someone broke in? I mean, did you have mail laying around, anything with your address?"

"My registration was out of the glove box."

Sharon sat back. "That could have been it. They got the address and decided to harass you some more."

Cora stood up and shoved in her chair.

"Let's get to it," she said. "I don't have all day, and Arch will be over pretty soon. I have to measure the broken window so he can cut a board to fix it."

"Hey, thanks for the coffee and sweets, but I can get this," I said, standing up, too.

"Archie will be very disappointed if he doesn't get to use his tools," Cora grinned, "and besides, he needs to feel like he helped. He's a lot more sensitive than you know."

Sharon stood up and came around the table to hug me. "That's what friends are for, sweetie. Where do we start?"

Although I did put up an argument it wasn't much of one. I was happy to have the help.

By evening the house was back in order.

Two carloads of full trash bags had been driven to the dump. Sharon and Cora worked alongside me.

I threw away all the food, condiments, spices, everything edible.

There was no way I could eat or drink anything that had been in the house. I couldn't even donate it for fear something had been tampered with. There was no way I wanted to chance being responsible for poisoning someone.

Archie had arrived with the precut piece of plywood, installed it on the back door with a lot of noise and such colorful language, we all laughed.

I left long enough to drive to the grocery store and get some essentials to restock the kitchen and refrigerator.

I kept the laundry going all day, washing everything, folding and putting it away. The towels from the linen closet, thrown on the floor, didn't appear to be damaged but I washed them anyway. Sheets, pillowcases, all of it.

Surprisingly the cats settled right in, playing several games of tag and floor hockey, until I shooed them to the next room.

When my bed was remade with clean sheets and quilts, they curled in their accustomed spots and promptly went to sleep, none the worse for their adventure.

"Well, if he gets through again he'll be easy to find," Archie announced when finished. "He's going to be the guy with a broken hand. That's half inch plywood."

We all admired his handiwork. Cora included a kiss, Sharon gave him a hug and I thanked him profusely. He refused to be paid, settling instead for Cora's promise of rhubarb pie.

I was not surprised my friends helped.

I was surprised by the absence of my neighbor across the drive.

I assumed I must have hurt his feelings when I refused to stay with him last night.

Maybe I did read too much into the situation.

The option, the one that kept sneaking in?

Maybe Tim was closer to the mark.

Every time I glanced that way his truck was gone.

All the time we had cleaned, removed and replaced I watched for something missing, something I hadn't noticed at first.

I came up empty.

My memory is like a sieve at times, holes everywhere, but to the best of my knowledge everything was here. Except for my computer, and the box of discs.

It would take hours going through my inventory sheets to determine if a book was missing, there were so many of them.

I had them off the floor and back on shelves but the organizing and inventory would have to wait.

Too tired to contemplate dinner I settled for scrambled eggs and toast. After I had eaten I made a cup of cocoa and settled into my clean living room.

There was one plus - the whole house smelled fresh.

I picked up the remote and turned on the TV, happy to still have both and chose an old black and white classic I had seen ten times or more.

I pulled the afghan around me and curled up on the couch.

FLASH

Hey, Muse, what's going on?

Do I have to explain it all or can you read my mind?

I can't read your mind, babe. Wish I could. How about the short version?

Someone broke into the house and trashed it. Everything. Even dumped the flour and the sugar for crying out loud. Most of it is back in place thanks to the gang. Looks like the only things I lost were my computer and a box of discs.

Inventory?

Haven't had time to start going through it. I have some of the hard copies. The majority is stored online and I'll need a computer to access it.

Insurance? Doesn't your aunt carry renters insurance on all three houses?

I think you're right. I forgot about it. Her lawyers will know. I'll give them a call tomorrow.

Should cover your computer at least. Anything else missing besides those disks?

Not unless it's a book I haven't gotten to yet. It's hard to remember what was here, you know?

I guess it would be.

He was quiet for a bit. I wondered if he was gone when he popped up again.

It's something small.

What? How can you tell?

Think about it, Muse. Why go through the oatmeal, flour, coffee, that kind of stuff? If you were looking for an elephant you wouldn't check the clothesline. It's logic. Either looking for something small or just plain vandalism. Added to jumping you in the park, I think vandalism is out. Someone is looking for something you have, something small.

You forgot my camera. That was stolen earlier, in the park.

That's it!

What's it?

The camera! They're looking for a picture, or a set of them, something you photographed.

That's silly, Tim. I don't often take picture pictures with it. I just photograph the things I buy, or things I might buy.

Or think about buying. You send a lot of pictures to Andy, right? To see if it's a deal or not, or if he wants it. Who else do you send pictures to?

My turn to think about it. I upload pictures of my books and other things I sell online. Those upload directly to sites where I sell. I upload everything to another site, an automatic backup cloud that holds a separate copy.

158

I don't see how it can be the online stuff. I never use my address. I use the P.O. Box as a return address.

You never use your picture? I mean a picture of you? No way someone could wait at the post office and follow you?

I don't put my picture on anything, why would I?

Okay, what have you taken pictures of lately?

Just the yard sales. The library sale. I did take some pics of the church rummage sale for their monthly bulletin but I emailed those direct to the church. That was months ago.

Good, we're narrowing it down. Is your calendar still there? In your office?

I think so.

Check the dates. See where you were the two weeks before someone broke into the truck.

Okay but why two weeks?

As fast as this has escalated, couldn't have been too long ago. Why would someone wait six or eight months to search the truck? Makes no sense. Has to be something more recent. We need a computer.

I can probably rent or borrow one.

Check with the lawyers first. Renters insurance might cover the cost of the rental. Plus they should settle that pretty quickly with the police report and all. Speaking of the police report, where was Officer Handy while this was going on?

He was on a case, Tim. He came by the Gem to let me know he was called in, long before my house was burglarized.

That's convenient. How do you know what time it happened?

Don't start! I swear you're jealous.

You may be right about that. Right now I'm not the problem. Does Sharon maybe have an old computer? Or an extra one?

That's a possibility. Unfortunately it's late and I am not calling her this time of night. First thing in the morning.

I was getting excited, too. I was pretty sure she would have an old one, or a laptop she could spare for a few days.

Good plan. Call Sharon, call the lawyers about the insurance. One way or the other we should be in business by supper time!

What am I looking for when I get a computer?

You tell me, Muse. Go back over all the pictures from the last three or four weeks and see what we have. It will give us a starting place at least. Get some rest. I'll talk to you tomorrow.

Sounds good, talk to you then. I am tired.

Goodnight, Muse. Consider yourself hugged and kissed and all tucked in.

Will do. Night, Tim.

Night.

Chapter Eight

I woke up in the morning with a crick in my neck and two cats glued to my side. The minute I moved Dave was ready to eat and making sure I knew it. Cletus stretched and yawned, remaining next to me. I stroked his fur and felt his purr vibrate.

Moving carefully, so as not to disturb him too much, I got up and made my way into the kitchen. Surprised to see the sun shining, I looked at the clock.

It was after eight, late for me. No wonder Davy was hungry.

I filled the cat's dishes with food and fresh water, started the coffee, and waited for it to brew. I hunted through the piles of unfiled documents in my office until I found the folder for my aunt's lawyers. Carrying it back to the kitchen I poured a cup of coffee and sat down at the dining room table.

Before the break-in I had all this information filed in order. Now it was just a jumble of papers, some folded at weird angles from being jammed into the folder, others from being stepped on.

I lifted a stack, spread it across the table and started sorting it.

I was still at it an hour later when there was a knock at the door.

Miss Ellie stood there, a covered dish in one hand, the leash to a yellow dog in the other.

"Good morning, Miss Ellie. Won't you come in?"

"I would like to speak to you for a few minutes, Tee. I assure you the dog will behave."

Standing aside I let her and the dog into the house. Cletus growled and disappeared as soon as he saw the dog.

Dave, on the other hand, immediately strode up to the dog and gave it a sniff.

The dog looked at the cat. Dave rubbed against the dog's front legs, his tail tickling the big head as he wove back and forth under it's chin.

The dog rolled its eyes towards Miss Ellie but held its sitting position.

Dave sat, extended his back leg and licked his foot.

So much for fighting like cats and dogs.

"That nice young policeman came over last night. He told me about your trouble. He asked me if I heard anything, or saw anything. I did not. Having gray hair does not make me deaf or stupid. If I had seen someone breaking into your back door, I have the common sense to call the police. However, as a senior citizen and a woman, I am not comfortable with this situation."

I was afraid she was giving notice. Just what I needed.

"I'm sorry, Miss Ellie. I know you would have acted."

"Well, it wasn't your fault, dear! I know that."

"What can I do for you?"

She had set the covered dish on the coffee table when she sat down. The dog had laid down on her feet, still eyeing Dave.

"I thought you probably wouldn't want to cook today. I made you a casserole."

162

"That's very kind of you, Miss Ellie. I appreciate it so much. Is there anything else I can do?"

"Well, Tee, it's about my lease." Leaning forward, she pulled some neatly folded papers from her purse.

In an attempt to forestall the inevitable I offered her coffee.

"No, thank you. I don't want to take up your time. I know you must have a lot to do, what with cleaning up and all." She opened her papers and turned pages until she found the one she wanted.

"Our rental agreement states on page three that I am entitled to one small pet, with your express permission. Greta is not exactly small," she said, indicating the dog lying across her feet. "However, I have been assured she will bark if she hears something. Under the circumstances I think we would both benefit from her presence. I am asking you to excuse her size and make an exception to the contract."

Relieved beyond belief, I reached to pat her hand. "Oh, Miss Ellie, it's not a problem, not at all. Greta is welcome. We can use a watch dog."

The yellow dog rolled her big, brown eyes at me and yawned.

"Thank you, Tee. However, I have a codicil I typed up, to amend the current lease. I would appreciate it if you could sign and date it. For my records. In case, you know, if something should happen to you."

She looked at her feet as she said the last.

I reached for her paper. She handed it over, indicating where she wanted me to sign. She even had a pen ready and held it out.

Taking it from her, I signed and dated the document and handed it back.

She still seemed uncomfortable although the dog had certainly made herself at home. Dave sat right next to the dog, batting its ears.

She stuffed the papers back into her bag and stood up. The dog stood with her, tail wagging gently.

"She is a very well behaved dog," I said, in an attempt to put her at ease.

"She appears to be, yes. I hope this will work out. I just got her from the pound."

Estimating costs of carpet replacement in my head, I just nodded.

"It may seem foolish to you, Tee, but it will make me feel better. She will be a companion for me, too." She stood and picked up the dog's leash. The dog just looked at her. Tugging, she got the animal to take a couple of steps.

Dave took a swipe at the dog's tail as she passed in front of him.

Making our way back to the front door, I opened it to show them out.

On the threshold she turned and patted my shoulder. "Please take care, Tee. I will call you if Greta barks, so you will be prepared."

I didn't have the heart to tell her Cletus was a better watch dog than any dog on the planet. I couldn't count the times his growl had told me someone was approaching the house. That growl was loud enough, coupled with his quick exit for the stairs, to tell me there was a stranger on the premises. I had yet to see him be wrong.

Miss Ellie and Greta made their way down the steps and across the lawn, headed for her house. The dog stopped and sniffed the grass but didn't squat to relieve herself, obediently following along with her new master.

I agreed with Miss Ellie. It would be nice to have another alarm system in the neighborhood. I just wasn't sure this was the right one.

I also found it a little curious that John had managed to get by and talk to her, to see if she had seen anything or anyone unusual.

I took my cup out to the kitchen and heard another knock on the front door. On the way to answer it I checked the floor to see if Miss Ellie had dropped something.

Opening the door I found the phantom detective on the porch, looking rather sheepish.

"I'd throw my hat in first," he said, "if I had a hat."

Stepping back I motioned him inside.

"Coffee?" I asked, leading the way to the kitchen.

"Love it," he sighed, pulled out a chair and sat down at the kitchen table.

Pouring another cup of coffee and filling my own gave me a chance to look at him. There were purplish circles under his eyes, his hair was rumpled, either from wind or running his hands through it.

There were dark smudges across the front of his denim jacket. His jeans bore the same kind of black smears, some darker than others, some just gray spots.

I put the cup in front of him and took a seat across the table, stacking up the legal files I was working on.

"Long night?" I asked.

"Oh, yeah," he said, rubbing his eyes and taking a sip of coffee.

What the heck, my momma didn't raise rude kids. "Want some breakfast? Toast?"

He leaned his head back and sighed again. "I would love breakfast, Tee, if it doesn't take too long. I have an hour to get showered, shaved, dressed and back to the scene." He glanced at his watch. "I already spent ten minutes deciding to come over here."

I stood up again and moved to the refrigerator, pulling out bacon and eggs. Getting out the skillet, I started the bacon.

"Big case?" I asked

"Found the boat," he said. "Or what's left of it. The wreckage washed into Jade Cove, or most of the way in. We've been over there since yesterday afternoon."

The bacon began to sizzle, filling the kitchen with that wonderful smell. I pulled out the bread and loaded the toaster, ready to push down the button when I started the eggs.

"Well?" I asked. "Did you find him? Dr. Hammond?"

"Nope. There was a fire on the boat, somewhere along the line. It's been burned but it's pretty much in one piece. We've got the hull pulled up on the beach, been trying to go through it. Hard to see anything last night, it was so dark. It took all afternoon yesterday to get it in, then most of last night to get it up to the beach. We stayed with it till daylight. The state boys will be here today, that's why I have to get back."

He held his cup out and I refilled it.

I turned the bacon. "Any chance he's in the wreckage?"

"Doubt it. We searched what we could see this morning. The boat wasn't all that big. The main cabin is

166

still intact, just burned pretty badly. Unless he's in a cupboard, or cabinet or something, which is still possible. People trying to hide from a fire will get into the most impossible places."

"So he could still be on the boat?"

"Like I said, I doubt it. Possible, yes, highly unlikely."

"Will this effect Mildred?"

"In what way? Millie is a lot tougher than people give her credit for. Plus, this has been hanging in the wind for a long time." He looked up at me. "She's going to get the money. That's direct from the insurance guy. Don't mention it, okay? That's not common knowledge, yet. With the hardship claim and all, the company is going to cut her a check. The house is in escrow, for a quick claim and that's almost complete. She should be set here pretty soon."

"I didn't know you knew her that well," I said. I noted he referred to her as Millie instead of Mildred, like everyone else.

"Mm," he said, with a yawn. "I knew them before the accident, slightly. The doc had some trouble at the office a few times before he disappeared. Nothing serious. A couple of break-ins, belligerent pet owners refusing to leave, that kind of thing. I thought I told you I knew them. Small town."

He rubbed his whiskers with both hands and finished his coffee.

"Be okay if I wash up?"

"Of course, go ahead, you know the way."

While he washed up I cooked the eggs, made more coffee, buttered toast and got it all on the table.

He looked better when he came back and sat down at the table. There was nothing he could do about his soiled clothes, the black streaks and smudges on his shirt and jeans, like the ones on the jacket he had pulled off and now hung on the back of his chair.

He had washed his face and run a comb through his hair.

"Oh, man, this is great," he said, digging in.

I sat down across from him with my own toast.

He ate hungrily, washing it down with even more coffee.

Finally he pushed back from the table and wiped his mouth on a napkin.

"That was awesome, Tee. I never had time for dinner last night, and then up all night, I was starving."

"More coffee?"

"Lord, no, I'm floating now. I have to get changed and get back." He stood up and pushed in his chair. "We have to get together soon," he said. "It seems like every time I try to get over here, something happens. I've been gone more than home lately."

"Yeah, I've noticed" I said, with a grin. "It's been kinda busy around here."

"I know, I know," he said sheepishly. "I did read the incident report. There were no other burglaries reported that night, no other disturbances. I really liked the part where you were running around without a shirt when the squad car arrived," he winked at me and grinned. "Sorry I missed that. I got that far before I was called off to deal with the boat."

"That's in the report? About me?"

He chuckled. "Not to worry, that part won't be a permanent record. The guys told me."

"Well, there's some good news."

He grinned at me. "Nice mental picture."

"I had to use my shirt to get the cats," I explained. "I put it right back on as soon as I got the cats in the truck."

"I would love to hear more but I have to get changed," he apologized. "These clothes are trashed. The wreckage finally showing up, trying to get it to the beach. Wading around in salt water and sand, climbing around a burned boat, not my idea of fun, believe me." He looked down at his soiled clothing. "I think these just go in the trash."

"Tell me about it. I thought about throwing all my stuff out, knowing someone had been pawing through it. I finally wound up washing everything."

He reached out one arm and pulled me to his side in a quick hug.

"Once this is over, we'll have dinner. Go out for a night on the town."

"I'll look forward to it," I said, but not willing to hold my breath while I waited.

I walked him to the door and watched as he jogged across to his own place. I had noticed the dark smears on his jacket and jeans when he came in.

I also noticed that his sneakers were pretty clean for someone dragging burned wood around in salt water on the beach.

Just one more contradiction.

I hated to admit it because I really like this guy, but Tim might be right. Time to back off a little, maybe start acting a little more my age.

I cleaned up the kitchen and dressed, having been in pajamas when John came in. Taking a last cup of coffee into my office I called my Aunt's attorneys.

Once I got them on the line, they were very nice and very understanding. The gentleman I talked to took all the information, including the case number the officer had given me, and promised to get back to me within the next couple of days. He assured me the policy would cover the loss of the computer.

On that bit of good news, I called Sharon at work, to see if she had an old computer or an extra one I could borrow. She had one not in use and told me to come get it, she'd have it ready to go by the time I got downtown.

This was shaping up to be a pretty good day, a nice change from the last couple.

~~~

I have never been a fan of insurance companies. Seems to me they make billions while fighting every claim. They demand their payments on time or else.

File a claim and they almost disappear.

Therefore I was pleasantly surprised Friday when the UPS driver delivered a brand new HP computer, complete with monitor and printer.

I signed for it and happily went about getting it unpacked and set up in the office. Even more surprising was the invoice that showed my Aunt Johnnie had sent it, not the insurance people.

It was easy to transfer all the files I had stored temporarily on Sharon's borrowed computer. I made sure I had everything off of hers, then packed it up to return.

My little office was back in shape now, with the new equipment up and running.

New computers are always so much faster than their predecessors. I started reloading all my files from the online backup site I used, grateful Sharon had talked me into the process.

While the new computer downloaded data, I locked up, and double checked the locks, before heading to the grocery store.

This called for a celebratory dinner.

Yet another silver pickup swung in behind me as I drove to the market. I made a mental note to find out what make John drove. Evidently silver was the leading color for pickup owners.

It wasn't John behind me, this was a guy with long hair to his shoulders.

I filled a cart quickly with the basics I still needed. Then, on impulse, I added the ingredients for chili and cornbread, one of my favorite meals. For the heck of it I threw in a carton of vanilla ice cream and a six pack of root beer.

By evening I had my clients files updated, including hard copies shelved in neat yellow folders, my inventory records and photos all loaded, and chili on the stove.

I mixed up a batch of cornbread and put it in the oven, looking forward to a home cooked supper. Even if I would be eating it for the next three days.

After supper and a shower I settled in with the new computer and a root beer float.

I was going over my last sales when I remembered what Tim said about the pictures.

Switching to that file, I started a slide show of photos, beginng with the ones from last month.

I always took two or more pictures per item so there were quite a few to sort through. They skipped past, one by one. They were of no interest to anyone else. All I used them for was reinforcing my memory, which I have already said is wonky at times.

Many of those flicking past on the monitor I didn't remember at all, which underscored my need to have them, in case one of my sales was questioned.

I paused the parade, and stood up to stretch. It was full dark outside. I switched on the outside lights, both front and back and went to make a cup of tea.

Settled back in, tea cup at hand, I started up the slide show again and watched the pictures slide by. It was fairly hypnotic and I found myself nodding. Enough for tonight, I decided.

FLASH

Hey, Muse, what's happening?

Hey, Tim. Going through those pictures, like you suggested. Haven't seen anything yet.

You got a new computer! Good deal. Insurance?

Aunt Johnnie sent it. She's going to have the insurance company reimburse her directly. This way I don't have to wait.

That's great news. So how's it going with the pics?

I started six weeks ago and I haven't seen anything. Makes no sense at all.

Any news from the cop?

Like what?

172

Did they find the vet yet?

Not that I've heard. The boat wreckage finally washed into a cove here. They got it up on the beach, what's left of it. John stopped by this morning and said it had been burned.

Ah, Johnny Boy. He hasn't been a lot of help.

Come on, Tim.

Okay, okay, sorry, Muse. So what else did he have to say?

Mildred is going to get her check. The insurance rep told him that much. Her house cleared escrow, according to John, so she should have that check pretty quick, too.

Did you find out how much?

Nope, didn't ask. I'm sure she told me $20,000. John said the agent told him $250,000. Big difference between those two. Either way, she got more than that for the house, even in a quick sale. She should be sitting pretty.

Maybe the old gal didn't want anyone to know how much she was getting. I wouldn't advertise it if it was me.

She's not old, Tim. She's probably my age. And she's very pretty. You may have a point, though, about the amount. She may not want people to know how much.

Shows good sense if she kept it to herself. Besides, you guys might not have been so eager to help her out if you knew she was getting a quarter million dollars.

I like to think I would still help.

You probably would, babe. So what did you find in the pictures? Anything?

Not a thing. I'm almost finished with them. I've checked all the jewelry and books I bought from Mildred. The glass ware I bought earlier that day went straight to Andy. The hall tree, too.

Hall tree? That the thing the cop helped with?

Um hum. Andy was out on a delivery and it wouldn't fit in my Explorer, so I asked John to help.

And that started the whole thing.

Not right then, no. It was a couple of days later the truck got trashed.

Close enough. I still say he has something to do with it.

Why? Think about it, Tim. Why would he have anything to do with it? He said he knew Mildred before Vince disappeared, at least he had met her before. He calls her Millie, though, instead of Mildred.

Whoa, back up a minute. He knew the widow?

Only through the case. He had to interview her, when it first happened.

Minutes passed. I wondered if he had wandered off again.

Any chance they hooked up? You said he was single, and now she is.

If they did no one ever saw it. I haven't seen any one at his house since he's lived there. Well, wait, his sister has visited a couple of times. No other women, though.

Well, we know he's interested in women. He's come onto you lately. Why not the widow?

I don't think so. I can't give you a reason, I just don't think so. Doesn't feel right. All the scuttlebutt around town was how close the Hammonds were, never any hint that they were not very happily married. In this town, if she had been involved with John someone would have seen something.

Could he have any effect on the outcome? Of the insurance claim?

174

I don't see how. He's not the only one on the case. Surely for that kind of money they would want verification from more than one guy.

Still something else to think about.

Why would he keep coming here, seeing me, if he was involved with her?

Good cover? Or good taste?

I think you're wrong.

About the cover? Or the good taste? Fair enough. I think you're wrong. We're even.

I sat for minutes, sulking.

How about the pictures?

What about them? I told you, I didn't see anything.

The only thing I can suggest is one more time. There has to be something.

Whatever it is, it can wait till tomorrow. I'm tired. I've been at this desk almost all day.

Okay, babe, get some rest. And hey, I'm just trying to help.

I'm sorry, Tim. I know. I'll start again first thing in the morning.

Night, Muse. Sleep tight.

I shut down the computer, making sure I saved my files, and went to check both doors.

Then I went upstairs to join the cats.

~~~

I was up early the next morning, determined to get a look at all the pictures taken last month. If Tim was right, there was something I wasn't seeing.

Comfortable in sweats, armed with fresh coffee, I planted my fanny in front of the computer and turned it on. There would be no sales for me today. I was on a mission.

Cletus stood up next to my chair and patted my arm with his foot. I reached down and scratched his ears and his chin.

"Not today, buddy. Today is a work day."

He squeaked at me. Dropping to all fours, he got in the cat bed under the desk and curled up. I could hear his rusty purr. He may never be a lap cat but he's been so much better since his ordeal in the truck. He might even be normal in time.

I checked the email first, to be sure I had no sales.

Then queuing up the picture file I started the slide show and sat back to watch.

It was almost hypnotic to watch them slide by. The majority were book covers, one after another. The monotony was broken up by the occasional quilt top or piece of glassware, then more book covers. I was beginning to think I had too many books for sale when the pictures from Mildred's yard sale started streaming.

I sat up a little straighter.

Opening a new folder, I slid each of the pictures over to the new file. I labeled it as Mildred, refusing to call her Millie. I checked that the pictures were copied into the new folder, moved it to the desk top and closed the picture file.

Clicking on the new Mildred file, I opened it and spread all the pictures across the screen in thumbnails. There were fourteen in all. Clicking on one enlarged it to full screen.

The first three were shots of the boxes of books. One picture of the two boxes sitting side by side, looking down on them, showing just the top layer in each box. The next two pictures were close ups, one of each box, showing the same covers in the top layers.

Carefully checking each cover I went over both photos. Nothing. There was nothing I could see stuck down between the stacks of books, written on the inside of the boxes, nothing.

The next six pictures were shots of the hall tree - each side, front, back, plus close ups of the front and back. Nothing. Unless someone wanted a couple of shots of oak wood patterns there was nothing to see in these.

Five pictures left.

Two of these were overhead shots of the shoe box full of jewelry, one closer than the other. Still nothing. Not wanting to list each piece separately, I had sold it as a lot to get rid of it.

The remaining three shots were more of the hall tree, taken from several feet away, showing its overall size in comparison to the bookcase on one side and a dresser on the other.

Nothing there either. All three shots showed the line of furniture set up near the house and a corner of the front porch. The foreground had caught part of the table, with Mildred sitting in her chair behind it.

She was squinting at the camera, her right hand on the cash box in the first of the three. Her head was turned in the other two, with her looking in the general direction of the house. Partly visible next to the garage was the front fender, door, and part of the cab of a silver pickup.

Two people milled around the yard, impossible at this angle to tell if they were men or women, taken from the back, with their heads bent over all that showed was jeans and sweatshirts. Another one up on the porch was definitely male, with big shoulders, long hair hanging over both sides. Probably the guy she said she paid to help her move the stuff.

I didn't recognize any of them.

That was it. If there was anything else in these pictures it was beyond me.

After I saved the file to the desk top, I sent a duplicate file to the cloud where I stored my records.

Once that was complete, I got dressed and packed up the computer Sharon had loaned me. When I had it loaded I locked up the house, checked both doors, and drove over to Kelly's.

Sharon was in her usual booth, fourth one down on the left. I grabbed a cup and slid in across from her.

She laid aside her crossword puzzle, folded her arms and waited.

"What?" I set my cup upright and looked for Sally.

"Haven't seen much of you lately. Busy?"

"Yep. Aunt Johnnie sent me a new computer. Trying to get all the files and records reloaded that were on the old one. I have yours in my truck."

"That was nice of her."

"She's really a nice person. This way she can wait on the insurance claim and I have a computer. I didn't realize how much I depended on it. I really appreciate the loaner. Got me through the week."

"Welcome to my world. The power goes out around here and I just about shut down the office."

Looking around I spotted Sally, two booths over, talking to Mildred.

"How's Mildred doing?" I asked, lowering my voice.

"Good, I guess. You heard they found the boat? Well, the wreckage of the boat. Her house cleared escrow, so she has to leave, although I think she's already moved. She filed a hardship claim with the insurance company and I'm pretty sure they are ready to settle."

"Yeah, I heard the insurance was going to pay."

"Oh? Where did you hear that?"

"John."

She smirked at me. "And how's that going?"

"John? Good. He's been really busy lately. That's why he skipped the Gem the other night."

"He does that a lot. Not sure I could deal with it." She looked at me for a minute or so. "Are you sure you want to deal with it?"

"It's the job. Cops are like doctors or firemen, always on call. They can't predict when they get called in, or how long they'll be out." I sounded like I was making excuses.

Sally finally joined us and filled our cups.

"What 'cha gonna have, Tee?"

"Sausage and eggs, scrambled, biscuit and gravy," I said automatically, stirring cream into my coffee.

"I don't know how you can eat like that and not gain weight," Sharon grumbled. "I would be the size of a house if I ate like you do."

I grinned at her. "I have to get back the weight I lost."

Having no argument with that one, she settled for sticking her tongue out.

"What about you, Sharon? You want anything?"

"I think I'll have the same."

"One check, Sally," I said. "How's Mildred doing?"

Sally made notes on her order pad. "She's doing pretty well. She's settling everything up, getting ready to move on. You know how that is, you hate to leave your home, lose all your things, and at the same time, it's moving on, a new place, and new people."

"Has she found a place?"

"She's staying somewhere around here till she gets her money, then she's gone. Somewhere back east, I think. Where ever her sister lives."

Sharon spoke up. "She got her check from the sale of the house. I gave it to her yesterday."

"Then she just needs the insurance check and she's out of here," Sally said. "I sure do wish her luck. She really loved Vince, and she still misses him. I'll get your orders in."

We sat in silence for a few minutes, sipping coffee.

I thought about how much I hated to move, and how lucky I was to be in my present situation. I made a mental note to call Aunt Johnnie and thank her yet again.

"Anything else going on?" Sharon leaned back, giving me her full attention.

I had tried once to explain Tim to Sharon.

She meant well, telling my doctors I was talking to myself, and got me an appointment with a shrink. I had no intention of telling her Tim was still around, let alone tell her he was giving me advice or to share his theories.

"Just trying to get things back in order," I said. "I did get all the accounting files up to date, so that's a plus."

"It will take a little time, sweetie. It's always surprising how much stuff you have that you take for granted. I think it's a disaster when I misplace an earring. Heaven help me if I lose my cell phone."

"I was lucky I didn't lose anything but the computer and a few discs. And the camera that was stolen. Still makes no sense why anyone would risk jail time for used stuff. If it was me, I would at least have stolen new things."

"They probably didn't know your stuff was that old. That's a chance you take with burglary."

"Come on, Sharon. Really? They went through the salt and pepper! What on earth did they expect to find in the flour? You helped me clean up that mess. Was there a real chance of money hidden in the cereal?"

"Diamonds? Rare coins? People hide things in the damnedest places."

"Uh huh. Like putting the extra key under the welcome mat?"

"I only did that once!"

"Yep, and now you hide it over the front door, on the sill."

"Not any more. I moved it."

"Under the flower pot or the ceramic frog on the steps?"

She fiddled with her coffee cup, looking around for Sally.

"Sorry, Sharon, but there is no way someone thought I had diamonds or rare coins. This town is small enough that you could ask around and find out there was nothing of real value. I drive a ten year old truck. I live in my aunt's house. I don't work, well not at a regular job. Heaven knows I do own a dress somewhere in the back of the closet but I rarely wear anything but sweatshirts, tee shirts and jeans. Who could possibly think I have something worthwhile?"

"You do buy all that used stuff, could there be something of value? Something you missed?"

"If it had value, it's at Andy's shop. My online sales are mostly used books, with a few pieces of glassware. What kind of burglar is going to know the difference in a five dollar used book and a hundred dollar used book? And who risks jail for a hundred dollar book if they even knew where it was?"

Sally brought our plates and distributed them. "Be right back with your biscuits."

True to her word by the time we completed the prenuptial arrangements with the food she was back with the biscuits and gravy.

"Anything else, ladies?"

"I'll be lucky to finish this," Sharon said, picking up her fork. "I only ordered it because Tee did."

Sally went back and brought up fresh coffee, filling both cups.

"How's the romance going?" She was looking at me.

"Me? I have no romance."

"Not what I hear. Talk around town is that Mr. Wonderful found himself a playmate." She shrugged. "You don't want to talk about it that's okay."

"Sally, look at me. I do not have a romance going. Got it?" I wasn't sure what I had going, but until I figured it out I was not going to invite even more speculation.

"Fine, just remember that when I don't buy you a wedding gift."

I watched her walk back to the counter.

"You know you won't win that argument," Sharon grinned at me.

"I live in perpetual hope."

"What is going on with John? There for a few weeks it looked like you guys might get together. Are you okay?"

"We're friends, Sharon. Who knows? We may be more one day. Right now, there's too much going on. With both of us. He's been on the case, Mildred's case I mean, plus other things. He's the only investigator we have here. I have all these things happening that I don't understand. It's all I can do to take care of myself and the cats."

"How about the doctors? Any tests coming up?" She slid the pepper across the table.

"Not for a couple of weeks. That stinking PET scan is coming up, and you know how much I hate that one."

Sharon nodded. "Yep, and I know you're going to be fine. You won this one, sweetie."

I smiled at her and dug into my eggs.

We finished up breakfast, and I paid our tabs, a thank you for the loan of the computer.

We left together.

On the sidewalk, Sharon gave me a quick hug. "Have to show a house. See you tonight?"

"Sure," I hugged her back. "Sounds good."

She turned right, to her office, and I went around the corner to the parking lot.

John was just getting out of his truck, parked in the slot next to me.

"Hey, stranger, I was just going to join you," he called as he moved around his truck.

"Sorry, just finished," I said, unlocking my door without really looking at him. I climbed in and shut the door before I looked at him. Once inside, I rolled the window down. "How're things with you?"

He stood next to my truck, leaning down to talk through the window. "Busy, busy. How about tonight? You going to the Gem with your friends?"

"Yep. If you get time, come on by. You know everyone." I adopted a casual air, trying to look like I didn't care either way what he decided to do.

He was back to those calculating looks, like he was trying to decide something. "I might do that," he said finally, straightening and backing away from my truck. Whatever decision he had reached could not be read in his hooded eyes.

I started the engine and released the brake. He double patted the door frame and backed away from the truck. With a final wave, I headed home.

Although we weren't spending time together, we sure ran into each other a lot lately. Curious. I needed a way to identify this particular silver pickup since there were apparently a lot of them in town.

Truthfully, I didn't even know what make of truck John drove. I tried to make myself a mental note to check his truck, then briefly thought about asking Tim to remind me. Not a great idea.

I chuckled most of the way home.

Chapter Nine

I entered the Gem with a light step that night. Nothing else had happened. I had all my files back. I was current on my businesses. I sold thre books and shipped them this afternoon.

Things were definitely on the upswing.

Archie and Cora were dancing, and gave me a wave as I headed back to our corner.

The usual crowd was there, everyone was talking and laughing, a typical Saturday night at the Gem.

I thought I saw Mildred at a front table with a couple of women.

That was odd.

I had never seen her here before.

On the other hand I didn't know who she was till the last few weeks. For all I knew she was a regular.

It was nice to be back and having fun, laughing and joking with everyone, dancing now and then. I kept an eye on the front door, watching for John, pretty sure it was going to be another one of those times he didn't show up.

Were we a couple? Heck if I knew.

I still had the nagging feeling Tim might be right. Something was fishy.

John was attentive when we were in public, paying me a lot of attention, laughing, even hugging me. Those little flirtatious things like touching my shoulder when he went past, shared smiles at someone else's joke, all those silly little things adults make fun of kids for doing.

On the other hand, he was known to move on down the road regularly, avoiding any kind of hookup.

How well did he know Mildred? He referred to her as Millie, admitted to spending time with her on her husband's case. That was to be expected. He was a detective. She was a married woman, or should have been at the time.

Am I just being jealous? Yes to that one, and I knew it.

Mildred was a beautiful woman, a lady, one of those polished and finished types that I was never going to be. Was there more to their relationship? I wondered if he had dinner with her while investigating, if he brought pizza over before the interrogation began.

What about his hands? It still bothered me that his hands were all scratched up the same time I was mugged in the park.

Tim said too much coincidence. Was he right?

I accepted another beer from Cora, still checking the front door.

Just as I glanced for the umpteenth time, John came in.

He held up a hand when he saw me, then went to the bar. He lifted a beer and sent me a questioning look. I held up my own to show I had one. He nodded, turned around and chatted for a few minutes with the bartender.

Whatever they were talking about gave them both a laugh before John wound through the tables and made his way to our's.

He said his hellos, dropped a kiss on the top of my head, and slid a chair over next to me.

"Hi, sweetheart."

"Hi yourself. You made it after all. I was about ready to give up on you."

"Don't give up on me, Tee," he said, looking into my eyes. "I may be late a lot, that's the job. That's not the choice."

Now what the heck? Is he flirting again or sending me a message?

Glancing up I saw that everyone at the table was watching us. Great, here we go with the questions again.

Cora caught his attention, asking about the burned boat. He turned to speak to her, sliding his arm across the back of my chair, his hand cupping my shoulder.

Sharon, on my other side, raised an eyebrow.

I shrugged. Who the heck knows?

After chatting for a bit with Cora and Archie, John cocked his head, then turned to me.

"Slow song, let's dance."

I stood up and let him lead me to the dance floor.

He was a very good dancer and I was getting better at following him. He pulled me in close to his body while we danced, I could feel the muscles in his arms tighten around me, his head bent close to mine, his lips close to my ear.

I heard him say my name, turned my face up to him and he kissed me, his lips firm on mine as we kept dancing. It had been a long time since I was kissed.

The instant I began to pull back, he lifted his head and put some space between us.

Even in the dim light I could feel all eyes on us as we moved around the floor.

We danced to another song before making our way back to the table, a nice safe dance with a proper distance between us. When we returned to the table everyone looked somewhere else, anywhere but us.

Carafes of coffee were being passed around and a tray of cups decorated the center of the table.

It was already late when John arrived and now most of the gang were leaving. Cora winked at me as she gathered her sweater and bag. She bent and gave me a quick hug on her way out.

As a rule we broke up by eleven or so and left the bar to the serious drinkers. Most of my bunch had worked all day and some of them would be working tomorrow.

None of us were really night owls.

"You ready to go?" John asked.

"Yes, it's late. I want to hit some sales tomorrow. I haven't gotten out much lately." I slid my chair back and stood up, digging in my pocket for my keys.

John stood up at the same time, tossing some bills on the pile in the center of the table.

I told Sharon goodbye and waved at the rest.

John took my hand and led me across the floor, weaving through the couples still dancing, and out the front door.

"Where you parked?" he asked when we were outside.

"In the back," I answered. We turned toward the corner, walking side by side.

He dropped my hand and held his out for the keys. I dropped them into his open palm and followed along at his side.

When we got to my truck, he unlocked the door, opened it, and stepped back for me to get in.

Whether the beer, the dancing, or just the plain idiocy of being me, I stood on my toes to wind my arms around

188

his neck, face tipped up to his, eager for another one of those kisses.

He caught my wrists and carefully tucked my hands back to my chest.

"Not now, Tee," he said, softly, and moved back another step, away from me. He dropped my hands and lowered his head. "Not a good time."

I felt the tears welling up, that terrible ache in your throat when you try so hard to hold back tears. I was embarrassed by my own actions.

"Oh, sorry, John. My mistake." My cheeks flamed. I could feel the blush, my throat still tight.

I climbed into the truck and slammed the door, twisted the key in the ignition, and gave the engine too much gas. The engine roared to life.

I put the truck in gear.

"Come on, don't cry," he said, his voice tight. He kept his hands to himself, his fingers stuffed into the tops of his pockets, looking back into the lot. "It's not you," he sighed. "It's me."

"Oh, that's a new one," I called through the closed window.

"Come on, Tee," he said, motioning for me to lower the window. "This is not the time or the place."

"Is there a time and place, John?" I challenged, letting the window down.

I knew I sounded like a shrew. I didn't care. "This seems to be a one sided deal here, so you tell me. When is the right time? Check your damned calendar and let me know, so I can check mine. I may be available." I felt my own temper rising. "Then again, I may not."

He folded his arms and leaned them on the frame of my truck window.

He took a deep breath and leaned closer. "You know as well as I do, if I start kissing you right now we're gonna be in the back of my truck in five minutes. I don't want that, not with you."

"Well, maybe I can resist you long enough to get home," I snarled.

"Tee, come on," he looked sincere, his eyes troubled. "That didn't come out right." He sighed, letting out another long breath.

I started to ease my foot off the brake. "Don't worry about it, John. I got the message. For your information, right now I don't trust you enough to be in the back of your truck. I'm kind of particular that way."

His hands tightened on the window frame. "You don't trust me? That's not fair. I have never given you a reason not to trust me." He actually looked hurt at the thought.

"You've never given me anything, John, except a ride. Oh, and a pizza. Forget it. I guarantee I will."

"Wait! Please? Can't we talk about this?" His knuckles were white where his hands gripped the window frame.

"So what is it your inquisitive mind wants to know right this minute?" I kept my foot on the brake, the engine running.

It didn't take a genius to know the moment had passed. Those dark eyes were hard to read on the best of days, in the shadowed parking lot they were black.

There might as well have been a wall between us.

"Why don't you trust me?" he asked finally.

"More than one reason, slick," I answered.

"Name one," he answered.

190

"Fine" I said, and took a second to think about it. I stepped on the emergency brake. "Okay, when you came over and had breakfast, when you found the boat . . . "

"I remember. What about it?"

"Well, your clothes were dirty but your shoes were clean."

I could see the confusion on his face.

"What the hell are you talking about? What shoes?"

"The sneakers you were wearing. Your clothes were dirty. Black smears all over, and yet your shoes were clean. If you had been wading around in salt water and sand all night your shoes would have been dirty, too. The same day I got attacked in the park your hands are all scratched up. And that's not all."

Once I got started it all rolled out.

"It seems that I run into you everywhere I go lately, unless we're supposed to meet and then you don't show up. When we're alone, we talk and eat and laugh, like old friends, nothing that could vaguely be called intimate or personal. In public, you do everything but pee on my leg to mark me as yours. You kiss me in front of all my friends and then slap me down if I want to kiss you." I had run out of air so I just quit talking, staring through the windshield.

He stood at the window, as still as a tree.

After a few long minutes, he raised his eyes and looked at me, drawing a deep breath.

"Ok, let's start with number one. I have more than one pair of sneakers. I always keep one pair in my truck, in case I should need to change them. Like, for instance, if I have been wading around in salt water and ashes. Two. It is fairly common for a police officer to get scratched up in the line of duty."

"And what about the other stuff? Kissing me on the dance floor, in front of everyone? That's pretty much a public statement. We're not teenagers, John! These are my friends. They think we have something going. They ask me about it. I don't know what to tell them because I don't know either."

He gave me another long look, folded his arms and leaned back against the car parked next to me. "All right. You want the story? I was asked to resign in L.A. That's why I left. A woman I was, well, involved with, filed a sexual harassment suit against me, and the department. Her friends backed her up. The department settled out of court, and I was asked to resign before I got fired."

He paused and glanced around the lot. "I was guilty of being involved with her but I never, and I mean never, forced her into anything! It came down to my word against hers, and the department settled the suit. I had to agree to two years' probation to get this job."

He was looking at his feet, around the lot, everywhere but at me. "There was an incident, here, last year," he hesitated. "Believe it or not, it was NOT my fault. Again. The girl involved in that one had a history of mental problems. I still got an official reprimand for that one, mostly because of the thing in LA. I have to be very careful with women. I can't take another hit on my career."

I waited, the engine of the truck still running. Not wanting to interrupt now that he was finally talking to me, I turned off the truck.

"That's also why I don't get involved with the women here. I dated a few, and the last one, the one I'm sure you heard about, was damn near my downfall." He straightened and came back to my truck, his hands tightened on the truck's window frame. "That was not my fault," he said through clenched teeth, "but it sure as hell didn't help my career or my reputation. So I swore off women."

I just nodded, wanting him to keep talking, afraid to move or make a sound.

"And then there's you," he said, looking at me for the first time in minutes. "I can't help but see you. You live right across the drive from me. I see in your windows at night, I see you working in the yard, going in and out of the house. You've been a fixture since I moved in."

He looked away again but his hands had relaxed, the knuckles not so white. "You're an attractive woman. You have some great legs," he gave me a small grin. "When you're working in the yard wearing shorts. Can't help but notice. I come home for lunch, or" he looked up at me again, "home to change my shoes, and I can't help but see you. And there's no guy around. That made me curious. Can't blame me for that."

He looked back down at the ground. "I ran a background check on you."

Now my hands were tight on the steering wheel, my own temper warmed up.

"You did what?"

"I'm being honest with you, Tee. You want the story? Here it is. I asked around, did some checking," again the small smile. "You're pretty well thought of in town."

"Thanks" I said, coolly.

He sighed again. "You wanted to know. I'm telling you." He was looking me in the eye now. "You don't act like other women. You never make a move on me, none of that coy crap, no baking cookies, inviting me to dinner, hanging around my truck," he shook his head. "Worse than high school."

He chuckled softly, to himself. "You seemed to be completely immune. That's intriguing in itself. When you asked me to pick up that furniture, I thought to myself, okay, now she's finally going to make a move. And you didn't. You simply wanted the use of my truck, nothing to do with me, personally. That was a blow to my ego. So, I had you make dinner and you know the rest."

"What do I know," I asked, just as softly.

He folded his arms, then leaned them on the door of the truck.

"Are you fishing here?" he asked, his face serious, "looking for compliments?"

"Come on, John. The way you've been acting you have to know everyone in town is talking about us. Is there an 'us'? When we're alone you act like we're old friends. Out in public you're completely different."

He met my gaze, held it. "I don't want one of those guys to ask you out. I don't like them dancing with you, buying you drinks, laughing with you. I don't want any one of them close to you. I don't want to share you."

I was stunned. My face must have showed it.

"You wanted to know? There you have it. I guess I'm jealous."

"Archie, Greg, all those guys, they're friends, that's all they've ever been," I explained. "We've known each other for years. We went to high school together."

194

He grinned at me. "I know. I told you, I asked around. You don't know how much some of those guys like you, want to know you better."

I felt my own jaw drop. "Are you serious?"

"Very. There's quite a few guys in this town who would like to get close to you, and it's not friendship they have on their minds. You give off this touch-me-not vibe and at the same time you have that come help me look."

"I'm not like that! I try to be nice to everyone!" I objected to this line of talk.

He chuckled again, his eyes warmer than they had been since we danced.

"I didn't say you weren't nice. You are. To everyone. You can do almost anything, you always jump in to help, you're funny, smart, and I told you," he winked, "great legs. What's not to like?"

He looked at me for another long minute. I could tell he was measuring me. Again.

With a sigh, he straightened up. "Now, as to number three, before you interrupted me, yes. I have been following you. Sort of. I know your schedule pretty well. I know your routine and your hangouts. You're pretty easy to find. And someone has been doing just that, finding you. So I've been keeping an eye on you myself. Plus, being honest here, I wanted to see more of you. So I show up where you are. As often as I can."

With another deep breath, he continued. "You are not the kind of woman to play with, there is nothing casual about you. If I get involved with you, it's for the long haul or someone gets hurt. I don't want to hurt you, and I sure as hell don't want to get hurt. Not again. And above all, I do not want anyone, no one, to find me making out in a parking lot."

I sat in the truck, feeling my cheeks burn, the tears back, close to the surface. I could feel his eyes on me without even looking at him.

"Anything else?" he asked. "Did I miss anything?"

I shook my head.

"Basically, I don't know if I am ready to commit. Not right now. At the same time, I don't want you seeing another guy, any other guy. Quite a dilemma, huh?"

I could think of nothing to say. I sat and stared through the windshield at nothing.

He straightened up again and stepped back from the truck, patted the window frame with both hands. "Have a good evening, Tee, what's left of it. I'll see you around."

With that he walked away, weaving his way between rows of cars and trucks, towards the front door of the Gem. His truck was probably parked up there.

I sat in my truck, in the dark, feeling the tears welling up. Handled that well, I thought.

His confession triggered my own concerns, brought my own doubts back.

Did I want to be involved? Make a commitment?

There is so much work with a relationship, whether it's personal or casual. When someone shares your life their feelings have to matter.

A joy shared is doubled, a problem shared is halved. My grandmother taught me that when I was young. Over my lifetime I learned the true wisdom of that statement.

I also knew myself. I never settled for bits and pieces.

If I was in I wanted the whole hog, from snout to tail.

I also learned that there are times in a relationship where you put someone else's feelings before your own. The importance of cooking when you don't feel like it, waiting on someone else when you're sick, picking up dirty clothes you didn't throw on the floor.

These things all come into play when you're committed.

All kinds of things come to mind when you consider sharing your life and time.

The cats were demanding in their own way. I doubted a fresh bowl of water and a full food dish would be enough for John.

His job was another thing to consider. Never knowing for sure when he would be home, or where he was, or even if he was safe.

Did I want to chance sitting up at night wondering if he was all right?

He made his position clear.

Now I had to figure out my own.

To be perfectly honest there was also the threat of cancer.

It could come back at any time. All the tests I went through every couple of months were precautions, check points, to see which one was winning the race – me or the cancer returning for another go.

Did I really want to add John to the mix?

He never actually declared himself. He explained a lot, he answered my questions, and at the same time gave me all the reasons he didn't want to get involved.

My mind, never my strong suite at the best of times, was misfiring like bad spark plugs.

I jumped like a jack rabbit when someone tapped on the window.

Thinking John had come back, I lowered the window, apologies already forming.

Mildred stood beside the truck.

"Tee? I hope I didn't scare you."

Well, you did, I thought.

"What can I do for you?" I asked, reaching to restart my truck.

"I saw John leave. I didn't want to interrupt you two."

Great. Now everyone had something more to talk about.

"That's okay, Mildred. Did you need something?"

"Well, I was hoping to catch you. I don't feel well. I was wondering if you could give me a ride home. I hate to bother my friends. They gave me the going away party and they're having such a good time. I saw you leaving, and I thought maybe you could give me a ride. I can pay for your gas."

It was hard to tell in the darkened lot but she did seem shaky, her fingers on the window jamb were trembling.

Flicking the switch to unlock the doors I motioned her around with my head.

"Sure, come on." Why not? Everything else tonight was out of kilter.

She walked around the truck and climbed in, clutching her purse.

"Seat belt," I said.

"Oh, of course, sorry," she fumbled around with the seat belt, clicked it, then readjusted her purse in her lap.

"Where to?" I asked, putting the truck in gear and backing out.

I didn't see John's truck anywhere in the Gem's front lot.

He was already gone.

~~~

I had to ask which way, since I had no idea where we were going. She indicated right, so I signaled and turned.

"Go out to Concord," she said. "I'm staying out there till everything is tied up. It's a bit of a drive but I had to get out of the house and I needed some place to stay temporarily."

Even better, I was now going for a ride in the country. All I wanted to do was go home, curl up with my cats, and have a good cry.

It was obvious there had been no kind of personal relationship in my life in quite a while. Surely, John could understand my concern, especially with all the weird things that had been happening. The break-in, the damage to my truck, being attacked in the park, things that I did not understand.

Mildred interrupted my thoughts. "I really appreciate this, Tee. It's very kind of you to go out of your way."

"No problem, Mildred. I hope you're feeling better?"

"What? Oh, yes, yes, I was just getting kind of shaky in there. It was nice of them to have a going away party for me. I didn't want to break it up because I felt bad."

"Perhaps you're coming down with something."

"Oh, I hope not, not with things beginning to work out."

"I hope you're not, too," I said, mainly because I didn't want to catch it whatever it was. "You've been through so much lately. Sometimes it seems like there's no end to the troubles."

"Yes, it has been rough. Vince's business was going downhill. This last year things have been so tight. We had to sell our stock, and with the economy we lost most of our investments. One thing after another. The lease on the office ran out, then they doubled the rent. We got behind on the house trying to save the business. Just keeps getting worse." Her voice clogged up with unshed tears.

"I'm so sorry, Mildred. But things are better now, right?"

"Better? How can you say that? I've lost everything! I had it all, Tee. Vince took me everywhere! We stayed in the best places, ate the best food and drank only the best wines. The women all wanted my Vince, but he was mine. All mine. You have no idea what it's like to be loved that way. You don't know. You'll never know."

Oops.

"I didn't mean to sound flip." I reached across the console and patted the hand clutching the purse. Her hand was like ice. She wasn't kidding about not feeling well.

I sped up and tried to say something positive. "The thing is, you have another chance. You can't dwell in the past. You're a lovely woman, you're still young enough to start over, maybe find someone else to share your life. With the money from the house and the insurance check you can go to all those places again. Travel, if you want. You're moving to the east coast?"

"What? Oh, yes, of course. My sister is in the east."

"There's a lot to see back there. So much history, great restaurants. You'll see, things will be so much better."

"You have no idea," she said.

After that poor attempt the conversation died.

We left town behind us and were winding through the wooded area east of town.

My thoughts stayed in town with John, with the mess I had created. Then I realized I didn't know where we were headed.

"Am I still going the right way?"

"Oh, I forgot. You don't know where we're going. When you get to Windmill Road turn left, up the hill. It's the old winery, on Bascomb. Do you know it?"

"The old Bascomb Winery? I thought that closed a long time ago."

"It did. The winery itself I mean. The buildings are still there. I rented one of the rooms where they did the wine tasting. They converted them into motel rooms. It's only short term. I'll be leaving next week."

"I didn't know they had rooms to rent. I'll have to remember that. Always good to know an out of the way place when family comes to visit."

"It's something new they're trying. At one time it was a very fashionable winery. My first job."

"Really? Working in the winery?"

"Yes, I did. Literally worked my way up. Started out washing the grapes, washing barrels, hosing down the floors in the cellar. Promoted to corking and packing and finally worked my way up to hostess. Hosting the tastings and special events. It was a big deal then."

She paused for a second, once again fiddling with her purse. She was beginning to make me nervous.

"That's where I met Vince," she continued. "He was at a community fund raiser where I was the hostess. I sold him two cases of wine that night. The funny part was he didn't drink wine, not then. He only wanted to keep talking to me. It was after we were married that he began to develop a palate." She took a deep breath. "From then on, we always had wine. He bought me the finest wines in the world. He became an expert, far more knowledgeable than I ever was."

The intersection with Windmill Road loomed up in the dark. I stopped at the cross street.

"To the left?"

"Oh, yes. You remember?"

"Roughly. Been a long time since I was out this way."

I made the stop and hung a left.

This was definitely an out of the way place. Dark as the inside of a tire out here, even my high beams were lost in the woods flanking the road. I mentally crossed off any thoughts of sending my family to stay out here. She must be getting a pretty good deal on her room.

After I made the left turn onto Windmill headlights flicked on, beside the road, and quickly pulled in behind me.

I didn't recall a car there when I made the turn.

Whoever it was pulled up close, right on my back bumper. The lights rode high, like a truck bigger than mine.

It was too dark to see the make or model, the trees so thick they cut off any possible starlight. I checked to be sure the doors were locked.

"There's a turn coming up," Mildred said, fidgeting in her purse. "Bascomb is just past the top of the hill."

"Which way?" I asked, slowing as I crested the hill.

"Only one way," she said pointing to the right. "It's a tight turn."

I was almost past the turn by the time she pointed and had to hit the brakes.

Mildred lurched against her seat belt, still clutching the purse.

The lights behind me slowed as I hit the brakes and swerved around us.

"Sorry," I said, backing a little and making the turn, keeping an eye on the rear view mirror. No lights. I felt better knowing whoever it was had gone on down the road.

Oak and sycamore trees closed around us, what looked to be blackberry vines thick between their trunks. There had not been much traffic here in a while. Branches brushed against the truck as I drove down the road.

"There's the sign," Mildred pointed.

I slowed to a crawl, making another tight turn into a leaf covered parking area.

The buildings were dark, no lights on anywhere. You would think they would put some kind of lights out for guests. The drifts of leaves covered the whole lot, completely covering any lines or directions painted on the asphalt.

Mildred pointed to the far side of the lot where several buildings grouped together.

Stopping in front of the nearest building, I turned to Mildred.

"Are you sure this is it? It doesn't look like anyone is here."

She was elbow deep in the perpetual purse.

Looking for her key?

I opened my mouth to ask if she wanted me to turn on the interior light when she brought her arm out and stabbed me in the thigh with something sharp, like a needle. It stung like a bee.

"OW! Damn, Mildred! What's that for?"

I slapped her hand away none too gently.

My leg hurt, a stinging sensation moving up my thigh.

"I'm sorry, Tee," she said. "You are not going to ruin this for me! It's taken too much to get here. Vince is not going to jail, not after all this."

"Vince? Vince is dead, Mildred! You're not making any sense!"

She laughed like a crazy person.

Behind me lights flashed on, lighting up my truck's interior.

I could feel my leg going numb quickly, a burning sensation spreading up and down my leg. I unclipped the seat belt and swung the door open, planning to jump out.

Mildred grabbed my arm, and tried to hold me back.

I pulled my arm and swung back, connecting with her face. I held on to the truck's door, and tried to use it to pull myself clear.

She grabbed the collar of my shirt, pulling me back, choking me.

My feet were out, clear of the truck. My tongue was getting thick, my arms and legs beginning to burn.

Forcing my weight forward I broke her hold and tumbled to the ground. I could not even break my fall.

I hit the ground hard, barely getting my head turned to avoid landing flat on my face. I tried to lift my head, get my legs under me. Nothing worked. It was like a shot of Novocain all over my body.

"Well, there you are," said a deep voice, somewhere in front of me. I managed to get my head around to see a big man, more of a big shape really.

Behind him a pickup glittered in the reflected light of his high beams shining on my white truck.

It looked silver.

"You just don't give up, do you? Keep your damn pictures. You're done now."

I couldn't make out his face. I felt long hair brushing against my face when I looked up. He was in silhouette against the backdrop of headlights. I didn't recognize the voice. I was sure it wasn't John, although the truck looked like his.

"I gave her the shot," Mildred called.

I heard her slam my truck door, heard her footsteps rustling through the dead leaves but I couldn't lift my head.

I couldn't move anything.

"Hurry, Vince, get her inside." This from Mildred.

Vince? The dead guy?

I couldn't feel my legs or my arms, nothing would move. Inside my head, I screamed for Tim, screamed for help, only nothing came out. My lips were as numb as my arms and legs.

"I gave her the shot," Mildred repeated. "In the leg."

"I see that, she's already under. I can deal with her. You take her truck, get it out of here."

I saw my feet lifted up but still felt nothing.

"I'll take it back to her house."

"No! The cop lives there. Take it back down to the crossroads."

Mildred argued. "That will point them out here! They'll find her!"

"Then take it back to town, just be careful no one sees you. Try to leave it back at the bar," he answered. "Make sure no one sees you."

While I lay there trying to move anything, without success, they kept talking, in low voices, more hissing than words. I couldn't make out all that was said.

Then Mildred came back into my line of vision.

She merged with the bigger shadow, making just one big black blot and then it separated back into two.

I could barely see her in the dark. I could hear her voice, a long way from me, but couldn't understand what she was saying. There appeared to be two of her, swaying back and forth and then everything went black.

I didn't even feel my head hit the pavement.

Chapter Ten

The next thing I remember was a head ache.

The worst headache in the world.

I tried to open my eyes. Blinking did no good, everything was black. There was nothing.

I closed my eyes and laid my head back down. Moving it made my head hurt worse so I tried not to move. It's hard to get your bearings when you are trying not to move.

Drifting in and out, I tried to use my ears, listening for a sound that would tell me where I was.

The only thing I could hear was a gurgling sound.

Water? Was I near a stream?

My mind was too foggy to remember.

After a while I tried opening my eyes again, without moving my head. Still nothing. Moving very carefully I managed to raise my hand and hold it in front of my eyes.

Nothing. I couldn't make out a thing. I used that hand to feel my eyes. No blindfold. Nothing covering my eyes. I was either blind or it was very dark.

My eyes closed and I drifted off again.

I don't know how long it was before I was aware again.

My head didn't hurt quite as bad this time.

Carefully rolling to my side I tried to see where I was.

My back was very cold. The floor I was laying on very hard and cold. Concrete?

With a slight shift of my head I attempted to look up.

Still nothing but the blackness. My hands and feet tingled, whether from cold or something else. I could move them, they did not appear to be tied or taped up.

I flexed my fingers and toes. They all moved.

Besides being cold, they felt wet.

I felt the floor.

It was wet, not my imagination. There was a couple of inches of liquid all over the floor. I hoped it was water. Whatever it was, it was cold and very wet.

I closed my eyes and turned to my ears for guidance, holding my breath and listening intently.

It sounded like water dripping somewhere, like a leaky faucet or rain.

Rain? Indoors?

Using my elbows and my arms I slowly pushed myself upright, pulled in my knees and got them under me. This time the pain in my head was not nearly as bad.

I sat that way for a while, slowly turning my head left and right. My neck worked okay but I still couldn't see anything.

What I could hear was the sound of water running, somewhere indoors. The sound more of a gurgle than a drip.

Someone filling a bathtub?

One side of my body, the side I had been laying on was wet. Evidently I had been laying in what I hoped was water for a while before I woke up.

Lifting one hand I cautiously sniffed and then tasted my wet hand. No smell, no taste. That's a good sign.

I wanted to sleep some more but the wet floor kept me from laying my head back down.

There was a funny smell to the place, an almost chemical, musty smell but it didn't seem to come from the stuff that soaked my clothes as I lay there.

To my left there seemed to be varying shades of dark. Not so much lighter as less dark.

I could detect movement waving my hand in front of my eyes but I couldn't really tell if it was by sight or by feel.

I kept flexing my hands and my arms. Everything seemed okay, just sluggish. My toes moved okay, my feet were okay, just cold and damp.

Whatever that wet stuff was it had soaked into my shoes.

I hadn't felt this kind of cold since I finished chemo.

My watch was the old fashioned wind up kind so I didn't know if it was working or not, unable to see numerals in the dark. Looking down made my eyes want to close so I looked up.

Nothing.

Reaching out, I felt nothing, not in front or to either side. The floor beneath the water was flat, concrete or cement. There were no walls I could touch.

From my knees I stretched my hands further out and still there was nothing in front of me.

I sniffed my hands again and still smelled nothing. Hopefully this was water covering the floor and not something worse.

It felt deeper than before. Was that my imagination? Or was the water rising?

Being very careful I got my feet under me and stood up, my shoes squished around my feet.

As soon as I was upright, I bent over and braced my hands on my knees, letting my head hang loose, hoping the dizziness would pass. After a few deep breaths, I straightened up. My head was a lot clearer, not as foggy.

I recited the alphabet.

So far, so good.

Bending my knees a little, I felt for my shoes. The water was over my ankles, covering my shoes completely. I thought that was roughly six inches. Hard to tell with my hands so cold.

With one hand held out in front of me, I started shuffling along, my cold feet slushing little wet sounds as I moved them.

What seemed like hours was probably ten or fifteen minutes when my fingers touched a rough surface in front of me.

It was solid and perpendicular.

I hoped it was a wall.

Feeling my way I got flush against the flat surface. Some kind of rough finish. Maybe plywood? My fingers were so cold I couldn't tell if the wall was wet or dry.

Gingerly, I felt my right thigh where Mildred had stabbed me. There was a knot, about the size of a marble, sore to the touch.

It didn't feel like it was bleeding. There was no tear in the leg of my jeans, no slit from a knife or scissors, only a small, sore spot.

Had to be some kind of needle. A syringe? A vet would have them on hand for animal shots. Tranquilizers? Did they give dogs tranquilizers?

They must. How else could they operate?

So I'm guessing I had been tranquilized.

Better than euthanized.

My head felt a little better. I still had the headache at the base of my skull but not nearly as bad as earlier. Other than the sore bump on my thigh, I seemed to be all right, other than very cold and wet.

I leaned against the wall, closed my eyes and counted to sixty before I opened them again, hoping my sight would adjust.

It was easier to get them open this time, the desire to keep them closed not as strong.

The shadows were less dense to my left so I started shuffling along the wall in that direction, keeping one hand on the flat surface. I kept blinking, struggling to focus on anything other than darkness.

I was wading now, the slush of my progress audible. In a few minutes I came to a corner. The wall I was following met with another. Same surface.

I turned so my back was in the corner and pressed into the rough surface, taking small comfort knowing nothing was going to get me from behind.

I bent down and felt for the water, the wet stuff, whatever it was. It was above my ankles. Had it been that deep before?

For the first time since I had started moving I rested my head against the wall, braced myself with my legs and tried to relax. I think I drifted off for a while. It was hard to tell.

What on earth was wrong with that woman? All I did was give her a ride, a ride she asked for! And who was the guy? I had a vague memory of long hair brushing my face as he bent over me. I remembered his voice being deep.

Was it the missing vet? Mildred had called him Vince. Surely, she would know.

I wished I had hit her harder when I swung back to break her hold.

Having the time to think about it I realized she must have been fumbling in her purse for the syringe, getting it ready.

I was set up.

She wasn't sick.

She was desperate.

I rubbed my thigh with cold fingers, felt the lump where she had stuck me.

I had a lot of experience with needles the past two years. I should have recognized it right away, although none of my nurses had injected me with that much force.

I made myself a promise that when I got out of here I would register my complaint directly - to Mildred's face.

And maybe her fanny.

Why me? What the heck had I done to her, or them?

I bought the hall tree and some books, a box of jewelry with little or no value. If she wanted it back she could have asked! Well, except for the hall tree. That had gone directly to Andy. Almost directly, I thought, with a little detour by my house.

John had helped me, used his truck to move it to my porch, where Andy had picked it up that evening.

Was there something there I missed? Andy had it, he had gone over it, and sold it quickly, making a nice turn around profit.

If there was something hidden in it surely he would have found it. He knew antiques, whereas I relied on him and his knowledge.

Was it John? Had Tim been right all along?

Things started happening to me the minute John got involved. He was never there when something happened to me, always showing up immediately afterwards.

I hoped Tim wasn't right about John.

There was still no light.

I was standing in the dark corner of nowhere, the only sound I could hear was running water. I realized there was only a faint burble now, and not as loud as it had been earlier.

Feeling around, my pockets were empty except for the card case in my back pocket.

No keys.

My key chain had a monkey on it that doubled as a miniature flashlight when squeezed. I wished I had it right now. This was one of those times where a cigarette lighter would be real handy, too, not just for light but for heat. My whole body was cold, not only my hands.

I wondered if my keys were around here, somewhere in the dark. I seemed to recall someone saying something about moving my truck. If that was true it would mean they had the keys.

Still feeling tired, I kept myself in the corner, using my stiffened legs to brace myself against the walls.

I closed my eyes for just a few minutes.

I don't know how long I dozed.

My head snapped up, smacking the walls of the corner behind me. The water was almost knee deep now, cold and climbing.

I rubbed my upper arms then stuffed my fisted hands into my armpits. I needed to get moving.

I was pretty sure I wanted to go to the right. I thought that was the direction I had been going when I found the corner.

It was still dark, although the area to my left still seemed a hair lighter.

I bent to touch the water, or whatever I was wading in.

I couldn't hear the water running any more, just the swish of it as I slid my feet forward.

I started moving again, still going right, now wading for real.

I counted to fifteen before my knee banged into something, something unsteady and shaky that felt like wood but was upright and curved on the sides.

Something bigger in the middle and smaller above and below. Some kind of metal band wound around the center.

A barrel.

Feeling carefully I found the rough circular top. With a little effort I got on top of it and pulled my feet up out of the wet. I could hear the water dripping from my feet into the water below.

Clutching my knees I rested there, my arms crossed on top of my knees, my head on my arms. My eyes drifted shut again.

FLASH

Muse, what's wrong?

Tim! Oh, Tim, man am I glad to hear you.

What's wrong? Talk to me, babe.

I lifted my head, gripped the sides of my perch, trying not to shiver.

Just stay with me, okay? I'm in some kind of mess here.

I'm here, babe. I'll be here. I've called to you a couple of times and you didn't answer me. Are you all right? What's going on?

Mildred, the lady from the sale, the vet's wife? She stabbed me with some kind of needle. Some man was behind us, she called him Vince. I tried to get away but I fell out of the truck, and I woke up here in the dark. I can't see. It's so dark and cold, man, it is so cold. And wet! I could hear water running for a while. Now I can't hear it but it's almost knee deep. At least I hope its water.

I was crying, my tears hot on my cold cheeks, so happy to have someone here, even a figment of a splintered mind. I was not alone.

It's okay, babe. I'm here, it's going to be fine. Are you hurt?

No. I don't think so. There's a lump on my thigh, where she stuck me. It's just so cold. And wet. She asked for a ride, and I was taking her home.

Back up a minute. You were taking her home? I thought the house sold?

It did. She said she wasn't feeling good and asked if I could give her a ride. When we were already in the truck she started giving me directions, out in the country, back in the boonies. Then she stuck me, and this guy was there. I fell trying to get out of the truck and then I woke up here, in the dark.

Easy, girl, easy. There's no light?

No. There's a place less dark, with like stripes. I'm trying to get there.

Where is she now?

I don't know. I think they left. They were talking about moving my truck, or something like that, I'm not real clear. My memory is really fuzzy. There's no one here now, but you.

All right, that's good, that they left. Now, do you know where you are?

I think it's the cellar of a winery, one that shut down years ago. Too dark to really tell. I can't even see how big the room is, or how small.

It's probably still dark outside. That's a good thing, means you haven't been out of it that much. Daylight may help. What else is there?

Barrels. I'm sitting up on one now, to be out of the water

Okay. More than one barrel? Can you climb up on them?

No idea, Tim. I found this one, and only wanted to get out of the water.

I am so sorry, babe, but you need to get down and feel around. See if there's more of them. See if they float. Anything. We need more details.

Reluctantly, I eased my feet down until I felt the floor.

The water was over my knees and if anything, it was colder.

Keeping one hand on top of the barrel, I made my way around it until I felt another corner.

There were barrels stacked against the wall, at least two high. Moving slowly, I felt along the stack. Another stack was beside it. They seemed to be stacked up all along this wall.

Tim?

Right here, Muse. What did you find?

This wall seems to have stacks of barrels against it. At least two high.

Be careful there, don't knock them over. What else?

That's it. The first wall I found was rough, like wood maybe. I followed that to a corner. From the corner I found the barrel. It didn't have another one stacked on it. I sat on that for a while, to get out of the water. Now, this wall seems to be all barrels stacked against it.

That's two walls then. What's on the third?

No idea, haven't got there yet. I'm almost across from where I started if the room is square. There's stripes over there of some kind, really vague.

Take it easy for a minute, then we'll go. Do you have any idea where you are?

Yeah, I'm in a dark room flooding with water. I hope this is water.

I know that, babe, I meant area, locale. Where were you when she stuck you?

Oh. Parking lot of the Gem. She asked me for a ride, said she was staying at an old winery, that they were renting rooms now.

Name of the winery?

I can't remember. Bishop? Bridges? It's not coming.

Starts with a B?

Yes. I know it, I just can't pull it up. I'm so cold, hard to think.

It's a winery?

I think that's what she said. I can't remember the name! It closed years ago.

What kind of wine did they make?

I don't know. I rarely drink wine so I don't buy it. Besides, my memory sucks.

Did you ever see their logo? On road signs or bottles?

I don't remember, I might have.

Think about it for a minute. Relax.

That's easy for you to say.

Look toward the stripes. Are they any brighter?

I turned my head to the left and looked in the direction I had seen the stripes. I closed my eyes, then blinked a few times. I could only see them if I looked to the side, with my peripheral vision. They wavered there.

Not really. They are still there though.

Can you count them?

Maybe. They're really vague. I have to look to the side of where I think they are.

What's the name of the winery?

Bascomb! It's the old Bascomb winery.

Good girl! See? You're doing great. Now, the stripes. Can you count them? Can you tell if it's a window of some kind?

Keeping one hand on the closest barrels I closed my eyes again and blinked. Whether it was my imagination or just wishful thinking they did appear a little clearer.

I think so. May just be me but I think they may be a little brighter. It's almost like they're floating up there, can't tell. If it's bars of some kind they're wide.

Can you get to them?

I can try.

The water was above my knees now. It was getting more difficult to wade forward. I moved my hand from barrel to barrel, keeping my balance, still moving forward.

Muse? Keep talking, babe, stay with me. What are you doing?

Moving. The barrels are on my right, I'm touching them with my right hand. The stripes are across from where I am.

Okay, keep going. I'm right here. And keep talking.

I can't talk and walk at the same time.

I've suspected that for ages.

Now you're a comedian?

Always, babe. How you doing? Where are the stripes?

Still across from me, more to the left now, not centered.

Should be a wall coming up. If you started at wall A and you're following another one, that's wall B. Go slow. I'm right here. Not going anywhere. Take your time.

I kept wading along, the water now almost hip deep, making it harder to walk. More of a swing a hip forward, then swing the other ahead, keeping my right hand on the rows of barrels.

I shuffled right into another stack of barrels. I felt them shift a little bit. Quickly I put both hands out to steady them and myself.

Muse? Come on, keep talking. What's going on?

I found the corner. More barrels. I ran into them. They're getting unsteady, not as solid as they were. It may be the water. It's getting deeper, harder to walk.

You okay?

Define okay. So far, so good. I can't see the stripes at all from here.

That's a good sign, I think. Now move along that wall. This should be wall C. Try to look up, see if you can see the stripes again. I'm right here. You can do this.

Yes, sir, I can do this.

That's my girl! I know you can, never doubted you for a minute. Just keep talking.

The water is still coming in from somewhere. It's getting deeper. I can't hear it but it is definitely deeper than it was.

It's okay, babe. You got in, didn't you? Gotta be a way out. Just keep going.

OW!

What happened? Muse? Talk to me!

Something sticking out of the wall. I ran into it. Something like a table or something.

Stop where you are and feel around. Take all the time you need.

I am, that's how I know it's a table, or a counter or something. It feels like metal, a table with high sides on it.

How high are the sides? Just a lip? Or is it a full side?

Side, about eight inches? Longer than my hand. With my wrist at the top, my middle finger is a little short of touching the bottom.

So almost like a box. How wide is it? Can you tell?

If I stretch out, kind of bounce on my toes, I can reach the other side. It's the same. Another side.

So it's like a shallow box?

Yes, except it's angled.

Slow down now. Angled how? Higher on one side from the ground? Curved? Take your time, sweetheart.

Okay, there's a six or seven inch edge straight down that meets a metal surface, like a table or a box. The box is maybe a yard across? Then there's another edge like this one. The whole thing is tipped up a little bit on my right. Feels like it's going up on that side.

Feel along your right. Does the angle get steeper?

Yes.

The stripes. Can you see them?

Yes, a little. Above me. Have to look to the side to really see them, you know what I mean?

Yes, I understand. Now the table, the metal box? Does it feel like a chute? Could it be some kind of chute?

Could be, yes, the angle gets sharper closer to the wall. I can't get past these barrels to see how far over it is.

Go the other way, see if you can get around the chute, and find the end of it.

Okay. I know one thing, this place is dirty. My hands are crusted with stuff, like dirt, and it won't wipe off, not completely. Kinda glad for the water right now.

Dirty hands are not the issue right now. Can you find the end of the chute?

Yes. Found it.

Now stand at the end of the chute and look back towards the wall. Can you see the stripes better?

Not really, they're still there but I can't tell what they are.

You're doing great, Muse. Go on around the chute, try to keep going around till you find the wall again. Slow. Don't run into something. Keep talking to me, tell me what you can feel.

Going around the corner of the table, down the other side.

Keep it slow. The wall should be right in there somewhere.

Found it, I think. There's something sitting along the edge of the chute, like a cardboard box, a carton. In the corner now. There's a wall of them, with this one right in the corner.

Is it a box? Can you open it?

It's a stack of them. I'm getting the top one down. It's heavy. Not too heavy to move but heavier than empty.

Be careful, don't tip it. Don't want something falling on your head. Try to keep it to the side so it won't fall straight down on you.

Its bottles. There's twelve of them, like wine bottles. Feels like there's cardboard between them, sectioning them. I think they're empty, there's no corks or tops on them.

Good girl, so far, so good. Work along the boxes and try to find the corner.

What am I looking for?

Another corner right now. You found two, there should be two more.

Keeping my right hand on the stacks of cartons, I waded forward, my left hand out in front of me.

Talk to me, babe. Try to keep talking.

What would like me to say, Tim? It's dark. I'm scared. I'm wet and cold. My hands are cold and dirty.

Yeah, dirty hands are the worst. Why I could never be a mechanic. How you doing? That wall should be there.

Found it. This one is like shelves, deep shelves. I can reach all the way back and feel another wall. The shelves are arm deep, so that's about two or three feet?

That's my girl. Now follow the shelves. Slow, there should be a railing coming up.

Railing? What kind of railing?

If you're in the cellar there should be stairs, somewhere, going up to the upper floor. You haven't found them yet, so you should be on the wall where they come down. Just go slow, don't run into them. Not sure if they run along the wall or perpendicular, so keep it slow. Don't want you to bang your head.

Got it! The stairs I think. The shelves stopped with a straight side, like a bookcase almost. Then there's a rough wall and now there's a railing, slanting up. I'm following that.

Hold onto that railing.

All right, found the stairs. Going up.

Slow, Muse. We don't want you to fall. Put your weight on the next step carefully, be sure it's solid.

They seem fine, I'm going up.

Damn it! Slow down!

The steps are fine, the railing is solid.

And what if there's a drop at the top?

Oh. Okay, going slower. Out of the water now. The steps are still dry.

That's a plus.

Here's the top, there's a little landing thing, and the railing is still solid, right up to the wall. A door! There's a door!

Can you open it?

No. It's locked.

Hang on, wait a second. Does it have a knob on it? Is there a lock you can feel? Like a padlock?

It's a push bar, across the door. Like a market or something, the kind you push the bar down and then push it open. It only gives a little bit then it stops.

Tears started to flow. To get this far and not be able to open the door was maddening. My hands were so cold it hurt to push on the bar and then the damn thing refused to open.

Don't cry, babe. We'll get it. Rest for a few minutes, get your bearings.

I have my bearings, Tim! I'm at the top of a staircase in the freaking dark and the door is locked and I can't get out. There's water at the bottom of the stairs and it's getting deeper by the minute. How's that for bearings?

All right, take it easy. I'm sorry, I'm pushing it.

You think you're pushing it? You should be in my shoes.

I wish I was. Believe me, babe, I wish I was.

What can you do I can't?

Not a damn thing. Now, are you ready to try something else?

Okay.

Hold onto the railing and back down the stairs. Literally, back down them. Don't try to walk down normally. Keep a tight grip on that rail. Be careful, please.

Going.

When you get to the bottom of the stairs, go to your right.

Right? I've been there. There's nothing there but that chute, barrels and a blank wall.

Trust me.

Well, get a piece of paper and write this down, so one of us knows where I am.

Way ahead of you, cupcake. I've been drawing a schematic.

And you're sure you want me to go right?

Right. Back to the chute. Sounds like a country song doesn't it?

Bite me, Tim.

With pleasure, Muse, any place you choose. Are you back to the chute yet?

How the heck would I know? Until I hit it, I have no clue.

There's no more light?

Nope.

It's close to daybreak. If there's a window or opening it should be showing up.

Found the chute.

Good girl! Now get back to the end of it.

There.

This is going to be the fun part. Can you climb in it?

Climb in it? You mean get up on top of it?

That's what I mean. That chute was built to get something down there. If you go up it, there has to be an opening of some kind. At least you may be out of the water.

You want me to walk up a chute? This thing is angled, Tim, like the slide at the playground only more so.

You never went up the slide? The wrong way?

Well, yes, yes I did. This is different. The slide wasn't this steep. Not to mention I was not soaking wet at the time and I didn't weigh a ton.

You weigh a ton?

Not now, Tim. My shoes and my jeans are soaked, full of water.

Okay, okay. How long do you think the chute is?

I don't know, pretty hard to tell.

Can you get up on it?

Trying. Okay, up on it.

Try crawling up it.

Too steep. I keep losing traction, sliding back.

Can you grip both sides?

Not enough to pull myself up.

Grip the sides and slide your knees up, see if you can use the buoyancy of the water.

It's pretty steep, not sure I can get up that way.

Okay, hang on a second. How about your feet? Can you brace your feet against the sides? If your knees start to slip, use your feet to stop.

Getting a good grip on each side I tried to slide my knees up, one at a time, right, left, right, trying to keep my feet tight against the outside edge. Out of the water the chute was dirty too, some kind of crust cover, not as slippery as it could have been, giving me some grip with my knees. Until my knees were coated with it, they got slippery too, like in mud.

How you doing, Muse? Keep talking to me, babe.

I can't creep and talk at the same time.

Sure you can. Hum. Hum a song.

Why? Have you lost your mind? I have enough to do right now!

Look who's talking. Keeps us connected, babe.

My hands are cramping, Tim. This is not going to work.

It will work. Just stay with it. Come on, you can do this!

I can see the stripes when I look up. They're on the wall straight up above.

Can you make out any details?

Not if I want to keep my balance.

Brace yourself, and look up. Is it a window?

Not sure. It looks like strips of board, like a crate or something. The damn thing is boarded up!

Okay, okay, don't lose it. Keep going.

226

My legs are tired, my knees are shaking and my hands are cramping. I can't do it.

You can do it! You keep going!

I can't, Tim. I'm going to lose my grip.

Come on, Muse. One at a time, left, right. You can do this. You can do anything. Look at what you've done. Hell, girl, you beat lung cancer. A puny little chute can't beat you. Get up there! Go! Go!

With Tim's constant encouragement, pushing and nagging me, I started to move again. It took a full ten minutes to reach the top of the chute.

There was a short flat space at the top and I managed to get my knee up on it, clinging there like a spider. I felt around with one hand, holding on with the other.

Tim, it is slats.

Atta girl! Are they inside or outside?

Inside. It looks like there's a window, with slats over it.

Can you see through the slats? Is there glass on the other side?

I think so, can't be sure.

Can you pull the slats off? Get your fingers between them?

Trying. They're pretty solid.

Can you get your balance, on that top space?

I'm lucky I haven't fallen already. Not enough room.

Check all the slats, make sure one of them isn't loose.

Tim I can only use one arm. I have to hold on with the other.

Okay, then, rest for a few minutes.

I can take a breather but there's not enough room to rest.

Can you check all the slats?

The one in the middle gives a little, not much, like maybe a nail is loose.

All right. Let go.

Do what?

Can you wiggle that slat? The loose one?

A little. Hard to get my fingers in the space between them. My fingers are so cold, they don't want to cooperate.

I hate to push, but you have to try.

Can't, Tim. No way to grip it to pull.

Push it sideways.

Wiggles a little bit.

Can you get a hold of the slat?

No, not enough room. Sorry, slipping.

With that I slid all the way to the bottom.

I reached the bottom a lot faster than I went up, landing in a splash. The end of the chute was under water, at least six inches covering the bottom of the chute.

Then I lost it completely and started to cry, tears of frustration not pain.

I had been so passive for so long, doctors and nurses telling me what to do, I did what I was told, losing any initiative. It all came back.

I wanted to lay here. So tired of it all. I could nap right here, let the water creep on up.

Stop it! You're stronger than that. Come on, Muse! I know you hear me. Turn around and face the end of the chute. Swing your legs over the end.

Fine. If I get out of here, I will never speak to you again.

You're on. Now, get your bearings again and climb out of the chute.

Okay, on the end, swinging my legs out. The water is over waist deep now.

Go to your right.

Back to the barrels?

That's it. There were some right at the edge of the chute.

Got it. It's a stack, I think, at least two I can feel. Bottom one is almost completely under water.

Pull it over.

Why? What if there are more of them? Three or more?

Stand to one side, close to the chute. See if you can pull the stack over.

Okay, trying.

Use your feet on the bottom one. Brace yourself and push with your feet, get your back into it.

Not working.

It will work! Come on, kick it! Keep kicking!

Finally the barrels tumbled over with a splash. Something brushed my shoulder as it went by. The air got thick, like it was filled with dust.

I started coughing, trying to keep my left hand on the barrel nearest the chute. If I fell I wasn't sure I could find this place again.

Muse, talk to me! Are you okay?

Yes! Give me a minute.

All right, take a deep breath. Relax.

I can't relax. I'm lucky to breathe! There's something in the air, dust I think.

Take it easy, babe. It's okay, I'm right here. Bend over, get your head down. Try to slow down, catch your breath.

I can take deep breaths but the water is too deep. My head will be under water if I bend over. Now what?

Can you feel the barrels? The ones that fell?

No. They're away from the wall. They fell out, not straight down. I think they're floating.

You're going to have to get to them.

Leave the wall?

Yes, go out, try to stay perpendicular to the wall. Shuffle so you don't fall over anything.

Here's one, on its side.

Did any of the boards break?

The sides? Let me check. Not that I can feel. Pretty big barrel though. Even floating the middle is higher than my head..

Good, that's what we wanted. Find the end of it and turn it towards you.

Okay done.

Is it the open end or is it sealed?

This end is open and the barrel is empty, thank heavens. Only a little water in it.

Wouldn't have fallen that easy if it wasn't.

It was not easy!

All right, all right. Save that for later. You have the open end of the barrel?

Yes.

Lift it up and drop it as hard as you can.

This thing is heavy. Being wet doesn't help. The water is pretty deep.

Can you get up on it?

No, it turns in the water. One side is sort of flattened. The metal ring at the top is loose.

Yes! That's great!

Why?

See if you can get that ring off, wiggle the wooden staves. Break one of those staves loose and we can use it as a lever on the slats.

How am I going to climb that chute again with a piece of wood in my hands?

Just get the stave, I'll tell you the rest.

I don't think this barrel is going to break.

Work the staves, the wood parts, see if you can get the metal ring off.

Okay, the metal ring is loose but it's sort of flimsy.

Yes! Pull it off.

I can't, Tim. It's like nailed to the other boards on the other side.

Push it inside, towards the center. The boards without the band. Push them to the middle if you can.

One is loose.

That's my girl! You can do this, babe! Keep pushing. Try pushing and pulling on it, see if it gets any looser.

After what seemed hours, the board I had gripped gave way. With a shout of glee I twisted it free and pulled it out of the barrel.

I got it!! I got one of the boards!

Good girl! Great job, Muse. I knew you could do it. Now, can you get back to the chute?

Okay, back to the chute with my board. I still can't climb back up this thing with one hand.

Not going to. Stick the board down the back of your shirt, all the way into your pants.

That is really disgusting.

This is the way you get out. It's not a fashion show. I promise not to look if that makes you feel better. Come on, babe, time's a wasting.

I felt along the curved length of the stave in my hands, being sure there were no nails sticking out or splinters. My hands were so cold I was afraid I would cut myself and never feel it.

With care I got the end between my shirt and my back and carefully fed it down till the end was at my waist. Pulling out the waist band, I managed to get it down the back of my jeans.

You ready, Muse?

As ready as I'll ever be.

Go get 'em girl. You can do it and I'm right here.

Climbing back into the chute wasn't easy with a board at my back but the water level was up over the chute so I could use the buoyancy of the water to get me back up on top.

I finally managed, and got my feet braced against the sides, using my knees, left, right, slowly climbing back up. My fingers didn't want to tighten. Every time I shifted my hands to grip higher, the board shifted from side to side down my back.

It took longer this time to get to the little shelf place at the top. More minutes were wasted getting on the shelf and gaining my balance when I got there.

I carefully slid the board up my back and out of my shirt, placing it cross wise on the little shelf.

How you doing, babe? You have to keep talking to me. You back to the top?

Yes, I'm at the ledge again.

Good girl. Now, use that board like a lever. See if you can wedge it between the slats.

Not sure I can get upright.

Hell yes, you can do it! Not a problem. And I'm right here, Muse.

I can't talk and do this too.

Just so you know I'm here. Do what you have to. You're getting out of there!

Clawing my way up, pressing against the slats, I managed to get both knees up so I could kneel on the flat space, holding on to the slats with one hand, feet dangling.

All the climbing had got my blood going again, my hands were not nearly as cold as they had been.

I felt for my board and got the end up close to where the slat had wiggled a little. It was tight, but I worked the board between the slats, leaning to the side so the board extended behind my shoulder.

When the board was as far in as I could get it from my precarious position, I put my shoulder against it and leaned into it. Then I caught it with my hand and pulled it back towards my shoulder. Then shoved with the shoulder, pulled with my hand. Very slowly the slat began to move, the board in my hands sliding between the two slats.

There was the sound of glass breaking. I froze, afraid the glass would fall back on me.

The board I shoved between the slats seemed to have shattered a window, and now went almost half way through the opening. Getting a good grip on my board I rocked it back and forth and suddenly one slat popped loose from the wall.

I almost lost my balance completely but the slat was dangling.

I slid the board over, behind the next slat in the row, wedging it to be sure it wouldn't fall out. Then I got a good grip on the dangling slat and pulled, rocking it away from the window.

It took several tugs, twisting it side to side, before it finally let go.

With a whoop I let it go and listened to it slide down the chute. It splashed.

I had no idea how far the water was up the chute.

Muse? Get it? Talk to me!

Yes! That's one. Now there's more room to get at the others.

Can you see?

There was light in the gap, still dark but definitely lighter than it had been.

Still dark out there, but I can see. There's buildings and trees.

You got it, girl! Come on! Get out of there!

I felt tears in my eyes just being able to see my hands again even if they were filthy and pruned.

With renewed strength I got my board and began to poke out the glass behind the slats. Fresh air poured in the opening, making it even colder on my wet hands and worse on my wet clothes.

Being able to get a better angle on the slats by sticking my barrel stave half way out the window gave me more leverage.

I went after the next slat with a vengeance.

Within minutes the second slat broke loose. Then the third broke in half. Pulling off the loose boards made an opening I thought I could manage.

Getting my head out through the opening I could see that I was close to ground level, no drop off to worry about, a dirty sidewalk maybe ten inches down.

With my head out it was only minutes until I worked my shoulders through the opening and then kicked my way clear.

I fell to the ground gasping for air.. Adrenaline lit up my system, my heart slamming in my chest.

I rested there maybe a full minute, then got to my feet. I was moving, even before I really had my balance, slipping and stumbling for the line of trees.

I just wanted to get away, put as much space between me and the cellar as possible. Stumbling along I made for the trees.

Tim! I'm out!

Way to go! I knew you could do it, babe! Now, you said there were trees. Can you get to them?

Ahead of you. On my way.

Reaching the tree line I tumbled down a little slope and crawled behind a couple of tree trunks.

Looking back the way I had come, I was down a slight hill. Only the top half of the grey building was visible through the branches. I couldn't see the broken window.

There wasn't enough light yet to see how obvious it was, although the light was growing every minute. I must have been in there all night.

Pulling in my feet I curled behind the biggest tree trunk, making myself as small as possible. My teeth began to chatter, my whole body shook as the adrenaline wore off and the cold returned.

You make it to the trees?

Yes, behind them now.

Okay, stay put. Wait till you see someone. Someone safe.

I don't want to see Vince and Mildred! They put me in there!

Relax, will you? Do you think I'd let you run to them?

Well, I hope not. This has not been a whole lot of fun.

Listen to me, sweetheart. Watch. Someone safe will come along. Then get the hell out of there. Get to the cop and tell him what happened. Got it?

Got it, Tim, but no one is going to show up out here. Not unless it's Vince. Or Mildred. This is the far end of nowhere.

Trust me, Muse. Someone will get there. Just stay back in the trees until the right one comes along. You'll know when you see them.

You leaving me?

I have to, babe. You're going to be fine. If you ever believed me, trust me now. You're safe.

Okay, Tim, but where are you going? Stay with me! I was kidding about never speaking to you again!

Stay safe, Muse. Watch for help.

I scooted back a little further, scooping up dead leaves around my feet and knees, trying to cover as much as possible, hoping even dead leaves would provide some kind of warmth.

Daylight had arrived.

Being up all night, the wading in water, the physical drain of that horrible climb, the fright, had burned all my energy. I was bone tired, cold, shivering again once I quit moving.

Scooting further into the trees, I rolled myself up as small as possible, with one arm cushioning my head. I closed my eyes for a few minutes.

The next thing I knew a police officer with the whistle from hell was standing over me.

Chapter Eleven

Once the police arrived I collapsed.

I tried to tell them what happened. My teeth chattered so hard my story came in bits and pieces. It sounded ridiculous even to me.

Another police car and an ambulance pulled up alongside the original squad car.

The first officer had given me a bottle of water. I drank half of it before I took a breath. He also gave me his jacket which I wrapped up in.

The cold was like chemo all over again. My jaws ached from clenching them, trying to stop my teeth from chattering.

The medical team had me sit up on a stretcher while they checked me over, wrapping me in a couple of thick red blankets. I kept the jacket, too.

I was filthy head to foot, soaked from the shoulders down, but other than a few more scratches I was okay. I was beginning to get used to sore muscles, scratches and bruises.

The EMT's insisted I go to the hospital and be checked more completely.

While the ambulance crew was cleaning up and repacking, ready to leave, another vehicle pulled into our lot.

A big silver pickup.

I fought my way from the stretcher inside the ambulance, jumped to the ground and grabbed the nearest officer, pointing to the truck, babbling.

"There! That's them!"

The truck slowed, then stopped right next to where I cowered behind the cop.

The door opened and John stepped down.

~~~

More hours in the hospital, being checked over.

The best thing was getting out of the wet clothes. And my hands getting warm, my fingers plumping back. I was afraid for a while raisin fingers was my new style.

Nothing is as miserable as wet jeans, nothing as good as hot coffee. I even got another shot. I hate shots. If I embroidered I'd give it up just because of the needles.

About the time I was ready to leave John came in, notebook in hand.

There had been no time to talk at the winery. The first officer left his car with his partner and rode in the ambulance with me, taking my statement on the way.

I went through the whole story a second time.

John asked a lot of questions, mostly if I had actually seen Vince. Like I would know him if I saw him. I couldn't identify his picture.

My memory was never trustworthy on a good day. After the night I had? I answered the best I could. "The only glimpse of the guy I had was a shadow. A shadow with long hair," I clarified an earlier statement. "The hair brushed my face when he bent over me."

"You're positive you heard her call him Vince?"

"Yes. That much I remember clearly. And she told him she gave me the shot."

He put down the pen and actually looked me in the eye. His eyes showed his concern. "How's the leg?"

"Sore. Everything is sore."

He grinned at me. "You think you're okay to go home?"

"I know I'm okay to go home," I answered. "All I want to do is go home. I want my bed and my cats. I may never leave the house again."

He looked at me for a long moment. I could see him considering something. "How about I bring over dinner?"

"No offense, John," I said, reaching to pat his hand where it lay on the bed. "I want to go home. The cats are enough company for now. And they're probably hungrier than I am. Thanks, anyway. Maybe next week?"

His face showed his disappointment.

"I appreciate the offer, I really do." I tried to soften my stance, not wanting to hurt his feelings.

I could almost hear the wheels turning.

"I can bring some cat food, whatever you need. Go to the store or make you some coffee. I want to be there for you, Tee."

Oh boy.

"John, that is so sweet of you. I really appreciate it. I do."

"But?"

"It's not for me," I said finally. "I'm too old for a boyfriend. I don't want a relationship. I love your company but that's it. I hope we can remain friends, good friends, but I don't think there's anything else for us."

240

"How can you tell? We've never had a chance, not a real one. Every time I try to get closer something comes up, something I can't control. Something that's not my fault either." His eyes were darkening as he spoke. "A lot of it is my fault, I admit that. Not all of it. Some of it I can't control, Tee. My time is not always my own."

"I don't blame you for that, it's your job. You're on call twenty four hours a day. I get that. There's so much other stuff."

"Like what? I explained to you about the scratches, the shoes."

"It's not you, it's me."

"There's a classic blow off line. I think I said that myself," he snapped.

"There is no line, John. I have thought about it. A lot. You are a great guy. I'm barely back on my feet. Look at what happened. I can't take care of myself, let alone someone else. For now, it's all about me. I have to figure out what I want before I can share it with someone else."

"And that's it?" His eyes darkened, his jaw set.

I could see he was not going to make this easy.

I nodded. "We're neighbors. We've become friends. Let's leave it at that. We can have supper together once in a while, watch a movie?"

Closing the notebook with a snap, he stood up and turned for the door. He stopped long enough to speak to someone standing in the hall and left without even looking back at me.

A nurse came in, bustling around the room.

"Do you have someone to call?" she asked. "You will need some clothing to wear. The police department required your clothes as evidence or something."

With a weary sigh, I picked up the phone and called Sharon.

~~~

I never knew who called the police.

Another one of those crazy coincidences.

I talked to Officer Chuck, who took the call. He said it was an anonymous call, someone reporting vandals at the old Bascomb winery. An ordinary concerned citizen calling. A car was dispatched and they found me in the woods.

I wondered if maybe Mildred felt guilty, leaving me to die, and had called in herself.

It took several days for them to track her down.

She was caught in Long Beach, California trying to board a cruise ship for Mexico. When they found her they found the missing Vince Hammond, with his long dyed hair and contact lenses, and took him into custody.

I saw the pictures in the paper.

He didn't look familiar. I was pretty sure I had never seen him before. He looked nothing like the pictures of Doctor Hammond that had been printed in the paper when he went missing.

Under questioning, it turned out I had seen him before.

I even had a picture of him.

A picture of him on Mildred's front porch.

The photos I took from the sidewalk, showing the size of the hall tree. The guy on the porch was Vince.

All the troubles started with me taking pictures.

Tim had been right about that although he was wrong about John. John had nothing to do with the crime, or Mildred.

Both Vince and Mildred saw me taking pictures. They thought I was taking pictures of Vince, that I was helping the cops or the insurance company.

With the insurance money on the line, Vince was not going to take chances and it was him that had knocked me down in the park and stolen the camera.

When the pictures were not on the camera, he kept looking.

The break-ins, my truck, my house, was him trying to find the pictures.

If they had left me alone, they would have gotten away with the whole scheme.

Another officer, not John, contacted me and asked for the pictures. They would need them for the trial.

I printed off a set and enclosed them with the original CD I had burned. I drove down to the station to turn them in.

I didn't see John, or his truck.

The bright note in the arrest was the healing scratches reported on Vince Hammond. They were reported as "animal scratches" and I took some comfort hoping it was my cats that delivered them. It was comforting to know I was not the only one who lost some hide.

My real luck had been their weaknesses. Neither had the guts to commit a direct murder, although Mildred gave one hell of a shot. It still had a small knot where she had driven the needle into my thigh.

Their decision to flood the cellar and leave me to die had actually saved my life, giving me the chance to get out. Mildred had said she worked there years ago, in that same basement, so she had to know there was another way out besides the stairs.

I will give them credit for one thing.

They did not turn on each other. I was pretty sure Mildred could have gotten a lighter sentence if she had blamed Vince for it all. Instead, she owned up, knowing in advance that Vince would kill the unsuspecting fisherman made her an accomplice to murder.

There too, the vet was unable to kill the man, instead cracking him in the back of the head and throwing him overboard. He didn't know the blow to the head had killed him. He thought he drowned. Like that made it okay.

The same in my case. Somehow they convinced themselves it was okay to drown me as long as they didn't kill me outright.

And people think I'm crazy?

There had been opportunities to take me out but neither wanted to be the one to do it. The final decision had been to lock me up in the cellar of an abandoned winery, turn on the hoses and leave.

They hoped by the time I was found there wouldn't be much anyone could identify.

I am grateful. Their decision gave me the chance to escape, a lot better chance than the fisherman had.

I spent a lot of time wondering if I wanted to rejoin society. The whole situation with John hurt both of us. So far, it had not been quite as attractive as everyone else painted it. I was vandalized, burglarized and almost killed.

I retreated.

I had my little online business, my books, my sales and my cats for company. Surviving the cancer experience made me comfortable being on my own.

There were good friends here, friends I could join if I got lonesome. Friends who would understand if I wanted to stay home and read. There is a lot to say for contentment.

While I do miss those little thrills and stomach flips at the sight of someone special, I don't miss the pitfalls when someone doesn't show up or call.

If I want to read all night and sleep all day, I am not responsible to anyone else. Except the cats.

They tend to yowl if not fed promptly.

~~~

I did lose something after the ordeal.

I haven't heard from Tim.

He was there the night I got home from the hospital, briefly, wanting to be sure I was, indeed, okay, and that I would be all right. He spent half an hour questioning me, until he was assured I was truly okay.

That was it.

Since then, nothing.

No blue flash, no ozone smell.

I wondered if maybe the fear or the adrenalin had snapped my mind back to normal, whatever that is. Maybe the two halves of my personality, or disorder, had somehow melded back into one whole. The last stage in healing, regaining full mental capacities? Had the cellar escape traumatized me enough to finally overcome the last of my side effects?

I don't know. And who can I ask?

I know I miss him.

We'd been through a lot together. I doubt I would have survived without his help. I know he is not real, he didn't call the police or anything, but he was definitely the reason I got out of the basement. That constant encouragement and nagging kept me moving, kept me awake, and eventually got me up that chute and out the window. It was his idea in the first place to look for a way out using the chute.

It may be a good sign, a sign that I am really healing.

~~~

In the next few week things settled down, although I still triple checked my doors every night.

That first week I refused to leave the house. The cats were thrilled that I slept so poorly at night we had to nap every day.

Sharon called regularly to tell me the specials at Kelly's as if I didn't know them by heart.

The gang from the Gem sent flowers although I wasn't sick. It was a nice thought, very kind of them. Maybe I did need to get back out there, resume what had become a pretty good life before Mildred.

Realistically, it was a fluke. How many people are killing their neighbors? Well, don't turn on the news and the number is not so high.

There was nothing the Hammonds could do to me now. They were in jail.

I lived in a small town, across the drive from a cop. I could go to the market and not lock my door. I had in the past.

I just wasn't ready yet, not comfortable away from home.

At the same time I was smart enough to know I had to get out there eventually, to retain my own mental health, prove to myself that I was really safe, really secure once more.

To that end I went to the grocery store yesterday.

That's progress, step one in my plan to rejoin the mainstream. That, and the fact that I was out of almost everything, including cat food. How long would Dave put up with canned tuna? Even Cletus had been pushing their food dish around the kitchen rather than eating, not being a fan of anything other than dry food.

Running out of coffee was the deciding factor.

I got my keys, locked up, double checked the back door, which still sported a plywood cover, locked up the front door and headed for the store.

When I pulled into the lot I noticed a silver pickup right behind me.

I freaked. My breath froze in my throat for just a few seconds, my heart dropping below my stomach. I slammed on the brakes and the truck barely avoided ramming me from behind, swerving around with a squeal of brakes.

Getting a grip on myself I managed to control my shaking hands and drive forward. I found an open slot and parked close to the door. The pickup that had almost hit me pulled in and parked a couple of slots up from me.

I watched from behind the security of my sunglasses and saw a tall, western type step down from the cab, glance my way and touch a finger to the brim of his hat.

I watched him walk through the double doors of the market. At least it had been a forefinger and not the middle one. Nice of him to acknowledge me, no hard feelings.

Then I started my truck, backed out, and drove to a different store.

I know it's silly. I am after all a grown woman and I have pretty much proved I am not crazy.

The silver pickup never did anything to me, not Vince Hammond's truck or John's. Neither the others I see everywhere, every day.

It was the sudden start when I saw one, the reaction without control. I even wondered if maybe John was following me around again but for what purpose? He knew where I lived and he had no reason to be on my tail.

Maybe Tim lost his place in my confused mind to a fear of silver pickups. Had I traded one aberration for another?

Let me tell you, I sure as heck preferred Tim to watching the rear view mirror every time I got in my truck.

I missed the feelings of security and warmth I had with him, the talks about books and movies. The silver pickups only gave me a start. Not a pleasant one.

I finished my shopping quickly, grabbed the basic necessities.

Approaching my truck with the bags loaded in a cart I looked around carefully, checking that no one was nearby, that there was no hiding place I had missed.

I made sure my windows were all intact, no silver trucks parked nearby.

You see? That's cautious, not crazy, and understandable after what happened.

I have to admit pulling into the filling station for gas, I went right on through when the same cowboy from the market was using the pump.

One of the nicest things about a small town is you know most of the people at least by sight. This was the second time I had seen this stranger in a few hours.

No more coincidences for me. In my heart I wished him well. Not his fault I now had a phobia about silver pickups. There was another gas station up by the freeway.

Next day I had lunch with Sharon, which meant a salad and fifteen reasons why I should be getting out more.

She doesn't understand and I can't explain it.

At the time it happened, I knew that I could die if I didn't get out. I could have drowned. The what-ifs took over the night time hours, and now there was no Tim to tell me I was being foolish.

It was the situation, the dark, the silence, the water getting deeper, the not knowing where or what, not being able to see. That kind of freezing, gripping, bone cold fear cannot be explained to anyone.

It comes in the night when you least expect it. It's worse in imagination than the actual ordeal. Like the chemo and radiation, only those who have been through it really understand it.

I had no doubt I would have cracked if it had not been for Tim. Or given up and huddled next to the door till my life floated away.

It's another mental scar, the kind that doesn't show but still exists. For me, it may never be over. In my own words, I possibly owed my life to a figment of my imagination. Oh, yeah, that's normal.

Focusing back on Sharon, and her insistence that I get back in the swing of things, I knew she meant well. She made a valid point.

The Hammonds were gone, yet they still had some control over my life and I hated it. I needed to get my life back, the life I had made with Dave and Cletus.

Cancer didn't beat me, I'll be damned if the Hammonds will.

To show my new resolve, when I got home and had the groceries unloaded, I unlocked the front door, released the chain, and stepped outside on the porch, enjoying the early evening air.

Someone in the neighborhood was barbecuing, the smell perfuming the breeze. Somewhere kids were playing, their laughter punctuated with sudden silences, like a game of hide and seek in progress.

Miss Ellie's dog, Greta, wandered up on the porch and sniffed my jeans, her tail wagging behind her. I bent and scratched her ears. She flopped down on my left foot and made herself at home. Together we watched the leaves rustle on the eucalyptus trees across the street.

Surely if the dog was that relaxed there was nothing here to fear.

There was a full moon rising. It lit the darkening street, highlighted the neighborhood with gilt outlines - the trees, the roofs, the cars.

The silver pickup across the street.

Was John parked over there? Glancing back towards his house I saw his truck parked in its regular spot.

Terrific. Two silver trucks.

When I looked back toward the other truck the headlights popped on and it slowly pulled from the curb and drove away.

It was too dark to see inside, to see who had been driving.

What difference did it make? Vince Hammond is in prison. So is his wife. There are hundreds of silver pickups and I seem to find one every time I step outside.

I wasn't hurt badly in the whole scheme. I lost a night's sleep, got a nasty puncture in my thigh, and got a really dirty work out. Big deal. There were no days and weeks of starvation, no torture, just a few more scratches to add to my collection.

My real concern is that I've traded in Tim for an irrational fear of silver pickups. I missed him these last weeks.

Jumping every time I saw a silver truck had no redeeming qualities. I wondered if a shrink could get Tim back for me. I bet no psychiatrist ever had to deal with a request to return the invisible friend.

~~~

I had a PET scan scheduled for today so I was up early.

I hate these tests. I always wanted them early, out of the way and done.

For those who haven't got to enjoy the PET, it involves stripping down to panties and one of those 'hi here's my fanny' gowns, being injected with some weird radioactive crap they keep in a lead lined box to protect the technician.

Then you sit for an hour without moving. No movement at all. No holding a book, no music in case you should tap your foot or finger, nothing, just sitting there in the gloom, listening to faint voices that never said anything you wanted to hear. Staring at the walls and curtains, counting the squares in the fabric patterns.

At the end of the hour, the attendant comes in and takes you to the chamber, where you are given ear plugs, stretched out on a narrow slab and told again not to move. Your head is wedged in place with sponges, shoulders rolled tight to your body and there you are.

The attendant hides behind a protective screen and the noise begins, because all these machines clank, roar, rattle and hum to their own rhythms so loud you can't think. Thus, the ear plugs.

Your body is shuttled back and forth through the machine's maw, a narrow tube that seems seven feet long, lit up like a third degree and the noise keeps rattling and banging while you pass back and forth beneath spinning metal rings that flash even more light.

It's a real hoot.

After twenty minutes or so, you shoot out the end and turn in your ear plugs and get dressed.

You don't get the results. That's left to the techs and doctors. You get your belongings back and are shown the door, by which time you don't really give a fig what they found, you just want a coke or a cup of coffee and to return to your place in the scheme of things.

Having enjoyed my couple of hours of fun, I headed home with a light heart. The year was ending on a high note, the next year looking good if I passed this test.

I had not seen a silver pickup for a couple of days, except for the one across the drive.

I decided to swing by the police station and see if John was up for coffee.

I knew I had hurt his feelings at the hospital. I wanted to make it up to him. We had not spoken since then.

While I didn't foresee a romantic relationship, who knows? No one can predict the future. Nothing wrong with a close friendship. After all, not everyone lives across the drive from a cop.

The officer on the desk recognized me. When I explained why I was there he picked up a phone, spoke a few words and handed me a visitor's badge. The gate buzzed, he gave me directions and off I went.

John stood up and gave me a cautious smile when he saw me coming. I thought that was a good sign. I realized I had missed having him around.

He motioned me to the chair in front of his desk, then sat when I did.

"How are you? You look good," he began. "Nice to see you out and about."

"Thanks, John," I smiled. "I am doing a lot better."

"What can I do for you, Tee?" He was giving me that measuring look again, that odd, calculating gaze.

He glanced at his watch, then looked back up at me.

"I was just in the neighborhood, thought I'd see if you wanted to grab a cup of coffee, maybe a doughnut?"

"Are you going to start the cops and doughnuts riff? You know I prefer peach pie." He smiled.

"Oh, no, that's not what I meant," I smiled, a little embarrassed.

John chuckled. "I would love to, Tee, it's just that I have a meeting coming up." He checked his watch again. "Maybe some other time?"

Looking down at my hands I twisted my keys. "Sure, John. I wanted to apologize. I know we got off track, and I acted like an idiot, but I really hope we can be friends" I said. "Maybe do dinner once in a while? I enjoyed that, and you are right across the drive."

He was considering, I could see it in his eyes.

"Maybe just coffee? Or a beer once in a while?" I wanted to make amends but I was a little tired of groveling here.

He seemed to reach a decision and sat up straight, checking his watch again.

"How are things at The Gem? You been by lately?"

"I haven't been there for a while, since, well, you know, the last time we were there," I finally admitted. "I'll be happy to buy you a beer if you want to meet up there again."

He was still considering. "Let's count on it," he said, finally. "How about Friday? I can swing by and pick you up or meet you there, whichever is easiest for you." He stood up and came around his desk to see my out.

"Sounds good. I'd like that," I said, standing up. "I'll meet you there, in case something should come up. I mean, I know how the job is, and all."

I stepped in and gave him a quick hug and backed away before he could return it.

"For the record," he said, with a little smile. "If something comes up I'll call."

I felt my cheeks warming. "Great! See you then."

I beat a hasty retreat, turned in my temporary badge at the desk and went back to my truck. I climbed in, started the engine and decided on a drive through for coffee, instead of going to Kelly's. Then it seemed silly to pay for coffee when I had some at home, so I turned the truck around and went home.

Chapter Twelve

Friday was another beautiful day, with a few sales to hit. I didn't find anything but I was out and about, reclaiming my life and doing what I loved.

Watching the time I swung over to Kelly's in time to catch Sharon for lunch.

She was in her usual booth, working a crossword puzzle, when I slid in across from her.

She looked up and smiled.

"Hey, stranger! What's up?" She slid the paper to the side.

"I was out at a couple of sales, thought I'd hit you up for lunch."

"You got it. Whatever your little heart desires." She pulled her cup closer. "It's good to see you. What have you been up to? Things going okay?"

I told her about the PET, the few sales I had seen, and she caught me up on her girls.

Sally came back, filled our cups and pulled out her order pad.

"Haven't seen you for a while, Tee. Everything okay?"

"Doing great, Sally," I replied, knowing that would be all over the diner by the time I left. "Fish and chips, please."

"Sharon?"

"I'll have the same," she said.

Sally paused, making a note on her pad, "You girls going to the Gem tonight?"

Sharon looked at me, and raised one eyebrow.

"Yep. It's Friday," I said. "I haven't been there for a while. Gonna put on my boogie shoes."

"Good for you!" Sally gave me a high five. "I may even join you tonight."

Sharon looked at her. "You? I didn't know you ever stepped foot in another establishment."

Sally thumped Sharon in the head with her pencil. "You don't know everything, Missy," she said. "I have a life, too. You might be surprised." She waggled her eyebrows.

"I have no doubt," Sharon replied and Sally wandered over to turn in our orders.

Sharon leaned forward once Sally was out of earshot. "Are you really going out tonight?"

"Yes, ma'am, I wasn't kidding. Already went by and invited John," I answered.

That got her attention.

"Wow! How did that go?" she said with another high five.

I slapped her hand and sat back with a grin.

"What did he say? Was he surprised? Do you think you guys will get back together?" Sharon fired questions like a political analyst on a third rate television show.

"There's nothing to get back to. I want us to be friends, Sharon," I said, holding up a hand to slow her down. "I really like the guy. I'm just not ready to take on a relationship, you know? Not right now. He's a nice guy, I like him, enjoy his company but I'm not ready to put his boots under the bed." I sighed. "I felt bad. The last time we were together, you know? I was kinda cold and I wanted to make it right."

"Hey, not my business," she admitted with a smile. "It was nice, there for a while, to see you with someone. Not alone all the time."

I remembered the one time I tried to explain Tim to her. She immediately wanted me to see a shrink, then stared at me for the next week. Since then I never mentioned him again.

Lately, without him, I was more alone than she knew.

"Here's a weird thing," I said, changing the subject, "I keep seeing silver pickups. Everywhere I go. Maybe paranoia? What do you think?" I sipped coffee.

"Hmm, well I guess that's possible," she said. "On the other hand, there's a lot of silver pickups. Probably the most popular color. I see them all the time." She gave me a guilty look. "To be honest, I look for them. To see if it's John."

"You do? You have a thing for John?"

"Oh, no! That's not what I meant."

Aha, too quick on the defense. I detected a flush along her cheeks, and made a mental note.

"I hope you two get together again. I just meant I look to see if it's him to wave at, or say hello. I check out every white Explorer to see if it's you."

"I see what you mean," I said. I know I checked every blue Lexus I saw to see if it was Sharon. "You're right, I do that, too. With me? I keep seeing the same silver pickup. It's the same guy driving it."

"Anyone we know? Maybe Archie got a new truck?"

"I'd know Archie. No, this is some new guy in town. Never saw him before and now he shows up almost everywhere I go."

"Small town, sweetie. Bound to happen." She looked down at her cup for a minute. "You haven't been out enough to attract a stalker." She smiled. "Plus, it is possible that a new guy, someone new in town, goes the same places you do. We don't have a lot of options here. Two grocery stores, two filling stations, two bars and one diner. You see what I mean? And if it's someone new, you tend to notice more. Does that make sense?"

"I guess you're right. I'm probably still a little paranoid."

Sally swept in with our plates and we both dug in.

~~~

Friday night I spent extra time on my hair, put a little curl in the ends, and even applied a little mascara. Amazing how much you forget how to do when you don't practice.

I went through my closet and found a blouse, something a little fancier than my standard tee shirts and sweatshirts. It was a little more feminine, although I kept my jeans and boots.

It was still light out at six thirty when I was ready to leave. I had my keys in hand, double checked the cats had food and water, checked the back door twice and made sure the front door locked behind me.

I looked both ways when I backed out of the drive. No silver pickups, not even a sedan. I hadn't realized I was holding my breath until I let out a big sigh, put my truck in gear and headed for the Gem.

I had an almost date, going to a place I knew very well. I knew the staff and most of the regulars. Time to get back to normal if there was such a thing.

My life had been quiet lately. The Hammonds were in jail, there was no one out to get me. My home and my cats would be safe and secure while I was out.

I turned guard duty over to Miss Ellie and Greta, who had turned out to be a great companion for the elderly lady, if not a great watch dog. I never heard her bark.

The dog often wandered over to lay in the sun on my porch while Miss Ellie worked in the front flower beds. I could tell when Greta was on the porch - Cletus growled and Dave jumped up in the window.

I drove into the parking lot at the Gem and circled twice, wanting a parking spot near the front. No more parking in the back. Although if anyone had seen Mildred climb into my truck they would just have assumed we were together.

Still, I didn't want to park in the back. I finally found a place up front.

Inside, they were all happy to see me, especially Sharon. No one mentioned what happened, where I had been. They all knew the story.

After the greetings, I accepted a beer from Archie and sat back to listen to the chatter and catch up on what I missed the past weeks.

The place was packed, standing room only for the latecomers. Looking around the room, I nodded to some folks I knew, smiled at others and waved at a few more.

These were friends - Sharon, Cora, Archie, Greg, all the regulars. The bar, the music, and the crowd all familiar. I knew the people and I was comfortable in this place.

I admitted to myself that I had missed this, the companionship, the comfortable atmosphere, even the smell of the place - beer and pizza.

When asked I danced a couple of times with the guys. I drank another beer and finally relaxed, for the first time in weeks.

A little later on, Sharon went to the bar and grabbed a couple more beers, slid one to me.

When she was back in her seat she leaned closer to me. "Don't look now but you have an admirer."

I looked toward the door, expecting to see John. "Where?"

"Hey, relax! It isn't John. There's a cute guy over there in that corner, by the juke box. I saw him earlier. He's been staring at you for a while."

I looked.

My breath caught in my throat. Was it him?

"Whoa, Tee! It's alright," she said, seeing my reaction. "You have got to get past this!" She patted my back. "It's all right. You're here, with friends, nothing can happen to you. Drink your beer. Enjoy the attention."

Mollified, I drank some beer.

She was right.

These were my friends. I had no doubt that they would jump to help if I was in trouble. This was a public place. A stranger couldn't do a thing to me, not with all these people around. Besides, John would be along eventually.

I was pretty confident he would show up. He said he'd call if he couldn't make it and my phone didn't ring. With a deep breath, and another sip of beer, I willed my muscles to relax. I tried to focus on the music, the dancers whirling around on the dance floor.

Sharon leaned in closer. "He may not be to your tastes, but that is one good looking guy. I wouldn't mind taking him for a spin," she winked. "That looks like my kind of cowboy."

I went cold all over, instantly. Like a bucket of cold water hit me.

"Cowboy?"

"Yeah, you know. Cowboy hat, longish hair, and plaid shirt. He's not driving cattle or anything," she giggled. "He's really handsome. And he's still watching you." She patted my back. "Not in a bad way, Tee, he's only keeping an eye on you, nothing weird." She grinned at me and winked. "You're a good looking woman, for crying out loud. Enjoy it! John isn't here yet and who knows if he'll show? We're all here to protect you. Go ask him to dance," she nudged me with her shoulder, looking to my right. "Go on. I dare you."

I tried to look casual, like I was just looking around the room and looked over at the juke box.

My breath caught in my throat.

It was him.

He was looking right at me.

Our eyes locked and held.

Then he lifted his chin half an inch, like a hello. He even gave me a little smile.

I felt my breath catch in my throat.

It was the same guy! I was sure of it! Why him? What are the odds?

I turned away, looked at the door. Where the heck is John when you want him?

Sharon leaned back and gave me a concerned look. "What's wrong, honey?"

"That's the guy!"

"What guy?"

"The one I told you I keep running into! Everywhere."

"The new guy? You think he's following you?"

"I don't know. I do know that everywhere I go this week I run into that guy. I know that's him! He's either in the same stores, or at the light, everywhere! I think he might even have been on my street. Driving a silver pickup."

Never subtle, Sharon turned around in her chair for a better look.

"That guy? The cowboy? He doesn't look dangerous. C'mon you're being silly. You want me to go ask him what's going on?" She made a funny purring sound in her throat. "I have no problem at all talking to that. Be right back." She waggled her eyebrows at me and scooted her chair back.

I pulled her back down in her seat. "No, don't do that. Just ignore him. He'll go away."

"C'mon, Tee, you should be flattered! Look at him, he's gorgeous. And he seems to be interested in you. You go talk to him, then. He certainly is not going to grab you in this crowd. You have to get past this, girlfriend."

She was right.

About a lot of things.

This is a small town. It's not all that unusual to see the same person a couple of times in the same day. This guy might be thinking I was following him. How funny would it be if he reported me!

Being new in town didn't mean he was a bad guy.

At the same time, it was beginning to give me the creeps.

Not his looks. Sharon was right. He was handsome. Magazine ad handsome. I was a little surprised the women hadn't dragged him on the dance floor by now.

Someone new in town could easily wind up in the same places I shopped or bought gas. We only had one main street through town and it was three blocks long.

Weeks had passed since I was in the cellar. I still spent more time looking in the rear view mirror than I did looking where I was going.

For what?

There was no danger. I was with friends. In a public place. In the town where I grew up and lived my entire adult life.

What's the problem?

A good looking man smiled at me.

I took a deep breath and checked the door again, to see if John had arrived.

Then it occurred to me there was nothing John could do if he was here.

The guy had broken no laws. He wasn't bothering any one, not even me. He, too, was in a public place, leaning against a wall.

It was me having the problem. Me, being uncomfortable with him watching me. What was I afraid of?

I beat cancer.

I beat Mildred.

I can face down this guy.

I stood up.

"You go girl," said Sharon, giving me a little push

As soon as I stood up he caught my eye and held it, watched me approach.

Up close, he was tall, a full head taller than me.

I looked up into smoky, blue-gray eyes that sparkled in the dim light, full of merriment. He looked like he was having the time of his life. Not the least bit concerned with me getting in front of him.

Well, fine, I thought, watch this. I got up right in his face, looked up directly into his eyes.

"Excuse me," I said, quite clearly. "Are you following me?"

He didn't even blink.

He smiled.

He opened his mouth.

He spoke.

"Hey, Muse."